EVERYTHING BUT THE TRUTH

EVERYTHING
BUT THE
TRUTH

CHRISTOPHER McPHERSON

ARSENAL PULP PRESS
Vancouver

ARSENAL PULP PRESS
103-1014 Homer Street
Vancouver, B.C.
Canada V6B 2W9

The publisher gratefully acknowledges the assistance of the Canada Council and the Cultural Services Branch, B.C. Ministry of Small Business, Tourism and Culture.

"Johnny Fear and Debbie Dare" appeared in *The Fiddlehead*. "The Children Who Sleep in the Jungle" appeared in *NeWest Review*. "Greek Coffee" and "Paranoia" appeared in *Wascana Review*. "The Food of Love" appeared in *Queen's Quarterly* and *Best Canadian Stories '93*. "Maudie" appeared in *Matrix*. "Hitchcock Diary" appeared in *The New Quarterly*. "The Warden" appeared in *Dalhousie Review*. "Falling" appeared in *Canadian Fiction*. "After the Fall" appeared in *Cut-to Magazine*.

Typeset by the Vancouver Desktop Publishing Centre
Printed and bound in Canada by Printcrafters

CANADIAN CATALOGUING IN PUBLICATION DATA:

McPherson, Christopher, 1952–
  Everything but the truth

  ISBN 1-55152-035-4

  I. Title.
PS8575.P472E93 1996   C813'.54   C96-910484-7
PR9199.3.M337E93 1996

CONTENTS

For Carolyn

Johnny Fear and Debbie Dare

MEETING IN DOORWAYS. Chimneys squeezing out smoke like dirty icing to decorate the sky. I was Johnny Fear and she was Debbie Dare, and every kiss lingered and left a stain.

There is a bridge at the end of time, but neither of us had a nickel for the toll. Her mother was a witch in curlers; my father had a tongue like an iron icicle. Meeting in the park, sharing a cigarette, crowding around it for warmth; her breasts left perfect dents in my dream. Milking the stolen moments, waiting for the cream to rise.

There is a bridge at the end. Meeting under it. Johnny Fear and Debbie Dare. Every kiss burned and left its brand.

———————

I had a job at Winston's warehouse, sorting tomatoes. The green, the ripe and the rotten. Deb was still in school, but failing fast. Across unimaginable oceans, and every night on the six o'clock news, Vietnam burned like the exploding future. At night my dreams were full of bright gleaming fruit, but every Beefsteak Beauty burst to slush in my hand.

I wandered the corridors of yesterday, looking for somewhere to plug in my amp. Meeting in back of the 7-Eleven, sharing a joint, crowding around our lust for warmth. Her breasts so cold they burned my fingers. A busted B-flat chord reverberating in the death of evening. Smog and jet trails.

I was playing bass guitar in a band, but we couldn't get a gig to save our lives. She was still in school, but she'd tired of kissing ass and left behind her B-plus average. We crowded around her burning homework for warmth. John and Deb. We promised nothing and believed all the things we never said.

———————

I sorted enough Beefsteak Beauties that winter to drown Moby Dick in Marinara sauce. To this day I have trouble eating a tomato I haven't known since it was a seed. One Friday night I borrowed my brother's car and spent part of my paycheque on a fifth of Southern Comfort and we got sticky and silly in the back seat. Our bodies scorched the vinyl seat covers; our clothes were a nuisance; every kiss left a trail of sparks.

Later she got sick and I scraped the paint off the fender, backing out of the alley. The rest of my paycheque. I dreamt tomatoes, but I woke still feeling her all over. Chimneys injecting the newborn morning sky with dirty dreams.

———————

I grow my own tomatoes now. I build houses for people with more money than me. I play a twelve string and write songs that tell everything but the truth about love.

The last time I saw Debbie Dare she had let some sailor get her pregnant and was thinking of changing her name. She was still in school, but she'd given up on failure and she had a year to go to be a dental assistant. Open wide, Johnny.

———————

We didn't really break up, or even grow apart. We just crossed the same bridge and wound up on opposite sides of the river. Every kiss leaves a scar.

The Children Who Sleep in The Jungle

MY VEGETABLES LOVE ME. We don't need each other. Love based on need is ordinary, inevitable, but it insulates the spirit. I slaughter weeds, persecute insects, and my vegetables are grateful, and give me their flesh for my salads and sandwiches. But we would get by without each other, if not thrive.

They love me for myself. I hide nothing from them. I am honest with my vegetables.

The snakes are harmless, beneficial even, but they frighten me a little. The frost is deadly, but my vegetables are not afraid.

———

Michael has gone with his pennywhistle and his juggling rings to a country where it never freezes. There are snakes in the jungle, carrying death like a rare gift, and soldiers who deliver it as routinely as junk mail. The nights are lit by burning villages. Michael juggles now for the children who sleep in the jungle. He writes to me; his letters burn my hand; they are onions to my eyes. But lately his letters do not reach me. The soldiers intercept them, to wipe the blood from their hands.

———

When Michael was a small boy, he found a snake in the garden. He ran to tell us. His father, mistaking his excitement for fear, killed the harmless creature with a spade. Michael wept. His father was shamed and embarrassed by his tears and told him to be a man. I wanted to weep, but I did not. I wish I had wept. I wish we had all wept together.

Now Michael carries a machete, to kill the snakes that move through the jungle more silent than regret. He kills swiftly, but still he weeps.

The children weep also, but they comfort him.

———

Michael needed me, and then he did not need me; he grew in me and I thought he was part of me, but he passed through my life on the way to somewhere else, receding always.

My vegetables hold the rain in leaf and stem; they suck the sunshine down into their roots and it rises slowly to warm them through the long night. Night belongs to the snakes and the threatening frost.

———

My father was a Presbyterian. My son is an animist. I used to like to sit and listen to God snore and mumble in the safe stark beauty of His house. But now I like to sit naked in the dark among my cabbages and carrots and listen to the snakes slide on dry bellies among the rows. They frighten me, a little, as God used to. But I feel the warmth stored in every cell of my vegetables. They protect me from my fear with their unselfish love.

They know the frost will come for them, and I will not be able to protect them. As they cannot protect me from death, which comes for me as inevitably as the frost. They accept death, as they accept the life which falls with the rain, and they help me to accept the things that frighten me. Like the snakes, which are harmless, beneficial even, and Michael growing away, and death growing close, the end of my growing season.

I know I am no longer young, or even middle aged, but I have not gotten over being a child.

My vegetables caress me gently with their dewy tendrils, and I shiver, as once I shivered when Michael's father touched me with his hard dry bricklayer's fingertips.

I think of the children who must sleep in the jungle. The blood of their parents cannot quench the flames which steal their homes, drive them into the terrible night, where snakes move, more silent than time, and strange gods live in the hollows which even the darkness cannot penetrate.

We are all just camping here. Someday we must all strike camp, and face night in the jungle. Michael plays his pennywhistle and the children wrap themselves around his knees and his kindness.

The snakes have no ears, but they listen with their tongues.

The young minister says he has come to ask about Michael, but I expect my neighbours have been telling tales, and he has come to see for himself. Before I let him in I put on my wig. The chemotherapy has played havoc with my hair.

Michael's father loved my hair when he was younger. He liked to brush it and braid it for me, or just to stroke it with his fingers. After his accident he drank too much, and changed. But still I am sometimes glad, when I must face the mirror, that he did not live to see me like this. He would have hated my wig. He grew away, too, but it was not just his accident, and the bitterness which settled in his twisted bones. I think I had never let him grow close, and he had to grow, so he grew away. I don't think I ever told him how much I liked it when he stroked my hair. How I missed it when he stopped.

The young minister holds his coffee cup away from himself, like a chalice full of sin. Perhaps he is afraid of the third sugar he put in when he thought I wasn't watching.

Your son is a very brave man, he says.

I want to tell him no, Michael is just a frightened little boy. But that would be playing into their hands. Besides, the minister is a frightened little boy, too, and perhaps it makes him feel better to believe there are brave men in the world. There aren't.

We all live in fear. Like the children who sleep in the jungle, we know the night is all around. No lock will keep it outside our doors forever.

The minister compliments me on my coffee. Perhaps God allows him to tell small lies. I wish he would go and leave me alone with my vegetables, and the spaces where Michael no longer juggles oranges and lemons, no longer looks at me with those little-bit wistful eyes. But he sits on his chair as if it is nailed to his rump. Finally he asks me about my health and I laugh and take my wig off. He almost takes a bite out of his coffee cup. I offer him more coffee, but the sight of my ravaged locks has reminded him of another appointment. Perhaps he is afraid that next I will take off my clothes and show him what the surgeons have left me.

When he is gone, I take Michael's last letter out of the drawer and weep, as I never did when he was there to take me in his arms and weep with me.

The cancer moves in me, silent as a snake. The doctors think they have cut off its head, but I know that was only another tail.

The cancer moves in me, a cruel wind in the desert places of my life. A secret kept too long untold. The desert places of my life are full of the bleached bones of my secrets, that now I shall never tell, for the ones I loved or hated, the ones I loved *and* hated, have grown away, have struck camp, have fled into the night.

Michael writes by the light of burning villages, but his letter will not reach me. The soldiers are frightened little boys themselves, but they don't want the world to know. They kill routinely to keep their secret. But they do not kill Michael. He moves like the shadow of darkness; he converses with the strange gods who brood in the hollows of the night. He kills the snakes before they strike, and cleans the blood from his machete on the broad leaves of the lianas.

Michael can juggle seven balls at once, but someday even Michael will drop the one that matters most. I knew before he flew that the cancer had taken root in me, and would spread, more persistent than the purslane and morning glory which strive to strangle my vegetables. But I said nothing. He yearned still for the Irish girl, Brigid, and for the children she would not bear him. I could not deny him the solace of the jungle, of juggling hopes in hell, that he might bide and watch me die.

When he brought her here, the first time, Brigid, I found her hard to swallow, like coffee that has been too long in the pot, like whiskey that has not been long enough in the cask. I understood later that she only struck at our vitals because she hoped to find our hearts there.

Michael could not cry when she left, and he would not speak to me of the desert that scorched him inside. It took the children to remind him of the place he had hidden his tears. It took his leaving to remind me where I had hidden mine.

It has been a good year. Rain and sun have shared the season between them. My vegetables touch me gently as I move through the rows, and rejoice as I pick them.

I sit before my magnificent salad and weep.

By the silent black waters of a volcanic lake, Michael teaches the children to skip stones. The pit-a-pats dapple the surface of the water with ripples which overwhelm each other. In the distance there is gunfire, and the children feel the ripples of war overwhelm them once more. They move close to Michael. The smallest child throws a stone in the water and it falls forever, falls to ring the bell in the center of the earth, and Michael laughs and hugs him.

I have never told these things to anyone. I have denied myself. I shall deny myself no more. It has been a good life. Joy and sorrow have shared the seasons. My body is riddled with treacherous cells, my heart is riddled with untold secrets, but I face my fear, and my spirit is with Michael, and the children who sleep in the jungle.

The frost settles silently. The night is all around.

I eat my salad.

Greek Coffee

ALISON PUTS HER TOOTHBRUSH in her purse. She dumps her school-books in the garbage chute and packs her flute and a change of clothes in her schoolbag. She buys a ticket at the bus depot.

The snow melts on the bus windows and Alison sits rigid in her seat and watches the droplets race across the glass. The snow snarls traffic, and slushes the gutters, but it covers the city with a sheen.

The sign in the shop window says:
    Wanted: Non-smoker, not too crazy, to share house with
    three others who hopefully fit same criteria. Reasonable rent,
    large room, good view of brick wall.
Alison copies the address and phone number on the palm of her hand. She asks a woman walking a dog for directions. The house is old and needs paint, and it stands beside an ugly brick low-rise apartment block, but it has a front porch and several oaks catch snow in the yard.

Alison mounts the steps, suddenly nervous, half hoping nobody will be home, though she has nowhere else to go. Someone is home. Before she reaches the door she hears a rattle and clash from inside, and then a short, blood-curdling shriek.

Alison stands and bites her lip, wishing she'd blown a quarter and phoned first, or slept in the bus depot, or tried the Y or something. Her lip starts to bleed. She hears voices from behind the door, and a flash of laughter, then again the tinkle and shush of metal on metal. An industrious ghost, mending his chain.

She actually turns to leave, but her small crisp footprints in the new snow stare up at her, and she suddenly sees herself retracing them, not just down the steps and up the walk, but back to the little shop where she saw the notice, back through darkening streets to the bus depot, back to the life she fled because she saw every step of it laid out before her, crisp and clear as footprints in new snow. Tasting her own blood, she turns and presses the bell.

A moment later the door opens and she is facing a tall cheerful boy in a white jumpsuit. Holding a sword.

Excuse me, says Alison. I saw your ad about the room.

Right. Come on in. Don't mind us; we're just practicing. I'm Zach; this is Stella.

Stella takes off her mask and switches her sabre to her left hand, offers her right. Zach and Stella are both tall and blond and good looking. They stick their weapons in an old umbrella stand, park their masks in the boot-rack and give Alison the tour.

A draughty stone fireplace in the living room, a leaky sofa, one lamp. The kitchen is bright and cluttered, full of plants and cats. Even before they climb the stairs to show her the large stark bedroom and the brick view, Alison wants to live here, in this warm house, with these silly people, as far from her father's frown and her mother's gleaming kitchen floor as the dark side of the moon.

Zach explains about the rent and arrangements; Stella explains about Zach. We're twins, she says, but Zach is twenty minutes older, and a boy, so of course he's insufferable.

Zach says, I guess we'd better take her to meet Zolte.

———————

Zolte is in the basement, brewing Greek coffee on his hotplate.

This is Alison, says Stella. She wants to move into Nellie's room.

Zolte looks at her, and his eyes go right through her, falling slowly, bright coins in a deep deep well. He is short and his hair is black. He is losing it on top and what is left is cut so short it bristles. He is dressed in black and wears a gold ring in his left ear.

Do you like Greek coffee? he asks.

I don't know.

Zolte lives in this basement, with his books. His black typewriter is so old you can look through it and see its works. The names of the popular letters are worn off the keys. Stacks of heavily annotated manuscript paper bury the battered card table which serves as his desk. Above the table and the bed hang large black and white photos of bearded men and spectacled women.

You are writing a book? she asks.

Zolte is writing the definitive history of anarchist thought, says Zach. But he's not dangerous.

Zolte pours the thick foamy coffee into two small clean porcelain cups. When he frowns he reminds Alison a little of her father, but when he looks through her with those eyes, she feels naked and newborn.

Stella and Zach don't appreciate Greek coffee, he says.

Alison takes the cup he offers and tests it tentatively with her lips. It clings to her teeth. It is strong and a little sweet.

Hey, she says, licking the foam off her upper lip. I like it.

She'll do, says Zolte.

The snow balances on branches and gathers in the bottoms of empty garbage cans, thick as sludge. Alison takes her toothbrush out of her purse and puts it in the bathroom. She puts her flute together and holds it for a long time, but doesn't play. Later, under the covers, she cries, and she doesn't sleep for a long time. Maybe it's the coffee.

———————

It's not quite so easy to find a job. Alison comes in, wet and footsore, and Zolte makes her Greek coffee and says, You need Grade 12 and four years' experience to wash dishes in this town. You should buy a good hat and blow that flute of yours on the street.

She doesn't. One night Zolte sits down at his typewriter and bangs her out an impressive, if fraudulent, resumé. Three days later she is desperate enough to use it, and the next day she gets a part-time job, waiting tables in a Chinese restaurant.

They didn't read it, she tells him, but I could see they were impressed.

———————

Stella and Zach are students at the university. Zach majors in chemistry; Stella is doing pre-law. She wants to be a judge. Both are on the fencing team. They usually get along, but sometimes they fight bitterly, when Stella leaves her dirty dishes in the sink before Zach brings a date home, or when his cats eat her plants. Alison gets used to the brief vicious exchanges which flare between them and pass as quickly, just as she gets used to the way Stella shrieks like a bird of prey when she scores a hit in fencing practice.

Zolte keeps a low profile. He works odd hours at an anarchist bookstore downtown, sleeps late and emerges rarely from the basement. Sometimes he will bake bread, or make a fire in the fireplace and sit in front of it for hours, drinking Greek coffee and prodding the embers.

Alison likes Zach and Stella, but they are involved with their studies, their university friends, their fencing, and each other. When she needs company, she ventures down the steep basement stairs and bothers Zolte. He doesn't seem to mind. He makes Greek coffee and talks to her of politics and travel.

He convinces her to call her parents.

You're working, now. You're settled. You have your own life. Sure, they can still hurt you, but you're strong enough to handle it. Maybe you don't have to keep hurting them.

———

Her mother's voice sounds very far away, at the bottom of a well, at the bottom of the sea, on another planet.

You hurt your father terribly. You might have called us, let us know you were okay.

I'm calling you now. I'm fine.

You're father hasn't been well, you know.

How are *you*, Mom?

You might have called. Or written a letter.

Sorry. Listen, I have to go, Mom. Say hi to Daddy.

———

One day Alison comes home from work, walks into the kitchen; Zolte and her father are sitting at the kitchen table. The brass ibrik is on the stove and the white porcelain cups sit between them on the table, a smudge of black in the bottom of each. Alison has never seen that look in her father's eyes. Like opening the door on January.

Zolte gets up and takes her hand. The world sways.

They told us it was only minor surgery, her father says, staring at the sludge in his cup. I didn't even take time off work to be with her. By the time they got hold of me at the office she was gone.

———————

Alone in her room, she thinks of her father, alone in his room. The bones of her anger lie under the museum glass, now. She will never forget the look in his eyes.

He can't forgive himself, and it is useless for her to forgive him. She thinks of her mother, alone in her box.

The windy night assaults her window; the brick wall howls. Zach and Stella are in Ottawa, fencing. Zach's cats are eating Stella's plants in the kitchen. In the bowels of the house, Zolte ignores the wind. His fingers pick letters from his brain and rattle them against the page like angry rain.

She wants to call her father, but she fears to hang her words in the cat's cradle of the telephone lines, where all the meaning can blow away in that wind, leaving nothing but the sting of what can't be said.

Sleep is a forgotten language.

———————

Zolte looks up from his words. Still, they dance in his eyes and she wonders if she is wise to try to come between him and his crutch.

I can't be alone tonight, she says.

———————

Strain the grounds through your teeth. Strong and just a little sweet. In Turkey they call it Turkish coffee, but only the tourists can afford it. The Turks drink *chi*. In Greece the tourists drink *Nescafé*. But not Alison.

Alison plays her flute in cafes and the Greeks buy her Metaxa and make her laugh, but she still can't forget the look in her father's eyes, that afternoon. Or the look in Zolte's eyes, that night. A deep deep well.

———

Foam gathers in the throat of the ibrik. In the yard, the oaks throb grudgingly into leaf. Zolte sits in the kitchen and plays backgammon with Alison's father. They drink Greek coffee and argue politics, raising their voices like any two Greeks in any hillside village in the islands or the Peloponnese. Alison's father is a socialist.

Sometimes they lower their voices and talk about her, compare postcards.

———

Alison sits in the Kri Kri Cafe, in Dzermiado, on Crete. She writes a postcard to Zolte:

Dear Zolte:

Spent the morning helping my friend put the sails back on his windmills. The snow is still deep on Dikti, but summer plays like a swallow over the Valley of Ten Thousand Windmills. People will never break their real chains, the ones that bind them together. Every time I drink coffee, I think of you.

Love, Alison

Paranoia

THE DRAGON LADY'S TOMCAT has pissed on my bike again. I have a little bottle of dreams hidden in my room, and I keep my Swiss army knife sharp. When I lived with the shepherds on Kythira I learned to cut, and one day, when the Dragon Lady and the Sex Goddess aren't around, I'm going to catch old Tom pissing on my bike and when he wakes up he'll have to change his name.

The Sex Goddess is the Dragon Lady's daughter, and she's out to get me. The Dragon Lady has dead white fire where her eyes have rotted out. She smokes like an electric chicken and pounds on the door and shrieks: Rent, rent, rent! and makes me sweep all the snow off my bike before I bring it into the hall so her fucking tomcat can spray it.

The Sex Goddess is jail bait that's been left in the trap too long. Her erogenous zones have minds of their own. I told her right at the start I thought I was coming down with something, AIDS, probably, but she just laughed. She already thinks I'm paranoid, so she doesn't believe my lies. She told me Mr. Milligan, who lived in my room before, told her the same thing, but she didn't believe him, either. No one is saying what happened to Mr. Milligan, but I imagine he's died of it by now.

All right, maybe I am paranoid. It's true I look both ways *and* over my shoulder before I cross the street. Yes, I get nervous around cops and people who are bigger than me, which happens to include ninety-five percent of the population over the age of eleven. But that's no reason for two perfect strangers in a brown Maserati to try to kill me.

Okay, I know you have troubles of your own. Your mother-in-law is poisoning your house plants; your lover is shagging the milk person; all your mail arrives wrinkled from the steam. But most every morning you can drag your butt out of the bed with a pretty good assurance that nobody is going to waste you before breakfast. Let me tell you, that's the kind of luxury you don't appreciate 'til it's down the toilet.

I started to notice a change a while ago. Catch a glimpse of the blank spaces out of the corners of my eyes as I was skiing on my bike in the back streets. I think they only own one snowplow in this town, and maybe they share that one with Regina. Mostly they just mix a little sand with the snow so it takes on the consistency of soft brown sugar. But if you approach it more like skiing than biking you may not wind up under a truck. You have to concentrate, but still sometimes, out of the corners of your eyes, you notice that the rough edges have been softened, rounded a little.

I am not a comic character. I flunked out of clown school. But lately my thought balloons are full of ampersands and asterixes and strokes of lightning.

I always figured I was something special. Just never quite sure what. I mean, there has to be some reason, out of all the people I could have been, that I woke up with myself. Legs too short, ears too long, hair that never stood no education. A voice in my head that has to peel the shining skin off every moment before it lets me taste the mushy bitter pulp inside. I've flown on the seat of my worn out jeans. I've led my life of crime as honestly as I could, and I've hardly been a perfect friend to every stranger, but I can't remember ever doing anything to anybody that they should want to hire two well dressed snakes in a brown Maserati to run me down on Avenue D.

I ask you—a *brown* Maserati? There is obviously something

wrong with these guys. Above and beyond the fact they got the wrong pigeon.

My bike saves me. I haven't always been kind to my poor bike. I've banged the old beauty down some roads that would have insulted a mule, left her chained at the mercy of dogs and small children, consigned her to the cruelty of railway baggage handlers. And she's let me down a time or two when I really needed a cold beer a hell of a lot more than a flat tire or a busted chain. But we go back a long way, and when it comes to the crunch, we'd rather not. My reaction time is good, but not as good as hers, and these bastards may be doing a hundred Ks in that shit-coloured car but we jump the snowbank like a frog with a firecracker up its ass. They never have a chance.

Maybe I am paranoid. But I don't like the feel of my thought balloon exploding. I keep to the sidewalks the rest of the way home, moving like the ghost of greased lightning through the rougher parts of town, and the trees are barely inked in before they are by me. I don't stop to sweep the snow off my bike either, and I don't pay attention to the Dragon Lady spitting nickels at me as I hit every third stair.

I've got nothing against this town only I can't find a job, and the rent's too high, and the winter twists its knife into you. The Dragon Lady likes to breathe fire, but her claws are dull, her fangs worn down to stumps from gnawing the bones of stony-broke boarders. The Sex Goddess is good for a giggle, if you can keep out of the way of her urges. As for Tom, he'd better enjoy his macho games while he still has all his equipment.

I was in love with a woman who lived in this town, once. I didn't come back to this country for the climate. Maybe cutting sheep and living on sour cheese and sleeping off the headthrob of a retsina haze, or working twelve hours a night with a bunch of timid

Egyptians in the leaping crackling sweltering glow of an olive oil factory, maybe that was not the most fulfilling life, either, but I could've stood it a year or two more for the privilege of riding my bike into the mountains and stealing oranges instead of getting my nuts froze off every winter.

But I met a woman who reminded me that I was not only a man but a person. A Canadian lady who made me homesick for the prairie winds which cleanse as they kill. She passed through my life more quickly than Canadian summer, but the feelings she woke lingered longer than winter in Saskatoon. It took me a year to save enough bread for the fare, but I put my bike in a box and flew.

I missed her wedding by a week and a half.

———

I'm not complaining. I'm still a person. Even if prospective employers look at me like I'm something they find on the bottoms of their shoes.

I bolt my door, try to remember if I've forgotten something. I don't think I fucked anybody's wife. I ran some dope once or twice, but I was always the one who got burned. I don't remember knowing anything about anybody they should want me to forget, permanently.

I have a good bolt on my door. I installed it myself, after the first time the Sex Goddess slipped into my room in the middle of the night and tried to overwhelm me with her abundant and enthusiastic flesh. I was taken by surprise in the middle of a dream and, slight and wiry as I am, I barely managed to slip from her massive embrace. I told her I had to run for a quick pee and locked myself in the can, shivering there reading back issues of the *Star-Phoenix* 'til dawn.

That was a long night, but not as long as this one. Sleep is present in the room, but won't get under the covers. Once I am sure they have come to get me, but it's just the Sex Goddess, checking, as always, to see if I've remembered to shoot my bolt.

If I had the bread to buy a Maserati, I probably wouldn't, but if I did it would be fire-engine red or the blue of the eyes of a Canadian lady who married ten days too soon. They must be professional hit men, if they aren't just figments of my imagination. Maybe one of them has a girl back in Sicilia with shit-brown eyes.

Morning, cold and bright as a magpie's eye, and the Dragon Lady's tomcat has done his thing. Your time will come, Tom, if I live that long.

The morning air freezes the snot in my nostrils. I would hide in my room, but the end of the month looms like a shit-brown Maserati, roaring up the calendar, and if I don't find some work and come up with some bread to throw into the jaws of the Dragon Lady, I won't have a room to hide in. Besides, after a night of nursing my paranoia, I can almost convince myself that I really *am* just crazy, not a marked man.

They are waiting for me outside the Canada Employment office. The bike senses them first, gets a shimmy in her front wheel and slips a gear. They are parked right there on 22nd Street, and they spot me just about the same time I spot them.

I've dared the traffic in Athens and Rome, played chicken with those big red London buses, even lived to tell of Montréal, but the chase I lead these guys through downtown Saskatoon is something else. They run that little piece of high-powered Italian shit through some places don't look wide enough for my old man to squeeze through without sucking in his guts. But I find the holes they can't squeeze through, scare the daylights out of some poor cat in a wheelchair, take years off the lives of a couple of student drivers and almost strangle myself in one of those endless scarves that is trying to escape from a cruel master. And I lose them. I think.

My breath is coming too slow for my heart; my thought balloon is swollen 'til it's squeezing the rest of me out of the frame.

I know this part of town, but it looks different. The last time I passed this way it was drawn more carefully, the detail was more authentic. I recognize the house I have learned to avoid, where a woman with Maserati-blue eyes lives with her new husband.

She works downtown as an aerobics instructor. She is in very good shape. She won't be home.

She is home. Her day off. She pretends I am a pleasant surprise, invites me in for coffee, but frowns when I wheel my bike into her carpeted hall.

You could chain it to the railing, she says.

It's not that, I say. It's just these two guys who want to kill me.

She just looks at me.

I know you think I'm paranoid, I say. I wouldn't have come here if I had anywhere else I could go.

I'm flattered. I'll get you that coffee and you can tell me all about it.

She is as bittersweet and inaccessible as ever. I know now, drinking coffee in her kitchen and telling her unlikely truths she pretends to try to believe, that her marriage is irrelevant. We touched in a place where strangeness drove us together. There we had in common the country we had left behind. Here, I am more strange to her, and she to me, than should be possible between man and woman. I have more in common with the Sex Goddess, with the Dragon Lady even. We belong in the same strip, if sometimes we crowd the frame. This lady doesn't even belong in the same section of the paper.

When our coffee cups are empty and only a stain remains, I beg her pardon and wheel my bike out her back door. I'd rather die in the alley, a victim of my own hallucinations.

———————

I take the long way home. I sweep the snow off my bike and try to concoct a story for the Dragon Lady, but just this once she doesn't emerge from her lair. She knows they are here, waiting for me in my room. She doesn't want to warn me by any gesture or word, but her very absence is a warning. And yet I am too weary in my soul and body, too drained to take the warning and jump another curb. I hit every stair on the way up, making sure to leave a muddy print. If they don't blow me away when I open the door at least I'll get to ask them what it's all about.

They don't blow me away. The room is empty. I close the door behind me. But I don't get quite as far as a sigh of relief. When I go to shoot the bolt it is gone.

Empty screw holes.

———————

Day winds down, a blade turning deeper in flesh. My thought balloon a desert. My knees are jellied, my fists are mist; I cannot fight, or run. There is no comfort in the encroaching dark.

I am weary in the marrow. Sleep in the room like a snake. I crawl under the bed and feel the coils constrict.

When I was a kid my mother would often find me sleeping under the bed. The dust mice were my best friends. But today I have no friends and the dust rats sharpen their teeth on my Maserati-coloured dreams.

The border between dark dreams and dusty darkness is unmarked, but I know I am awake. Someone is in the room. The Sex Goddess? No, I cannot smell lust, only leather and Old Spice and shoe polish. One of them has a penlight; I expect they both have knives. The one with the light comes to the head of the bed.

Asterix, ampersand, exclamation point, he says, his voice thin and sharpened to a razor edge.

The other laughs and his laughter is so cold I can feel it fall to the floor with a clunk and my toes go numb. We wait, he says.

They take off their shoes, hang their suit jackets on my one chair. They put something on the bed table, their silenced guns and switchblades, probably. They stretch out on the bed. They wait.

I will not sneeze. Not if the dust rats crawl up my nose and gnaw on the sneeze center in my brain. I will not clear my throat, though sandstorms erode my tonsils. I will not sleep, perchance to snore, though the serpent swallows me whole.

———

The Sex Goddess moves very quietly, for her size. Her nightgown drifts to the floor like an exhausted ghost. If she is startled to find two of me, she is not as startled as my killers. But her desire is more than a match for them. She removed the bolt from my door, and all day she has been stroking her anticipation. In moments their confusion has been smothered in her flesh, and I am assaulted in my dustbound sanctuary by bedsprings more brutal than the sea.

I've been beaten up before, but never with such relentless, untiring enthusiasm. The ebb and flow of their triple lust is a rhythmic storm that threatens to outlast the endless night. By the time they finally whimper into exhaustion, I am black and blue all over.

The Sex Goddess slips from the room as quietly as she had come, wriggling back into her nightie, giggling and steaming just a little. She leaves my would-be killers spent and dreaming of gentle assassinations.

I feel like I've been over Niagara without benefit of a barrel. My nose must be broken in three places. I wriggle out from under the bed. Clothes are scattered over the bed and the floor and the table. I try to brush some of the dust off my jeans but it hurts too much.

Enough dawn has stippled the frosty window for me to see them clearly. Two ordinary naked killers, asleep in a single bed. They look harmless enough, but the silenced .38 on the bed table has a sinister look to it.

I pick it up. I imagine I could figure out how it works, but I'd rather not.

The bottle of dreams is still in the back of my underwear drawer. This guy I met, a student, mixed it up for me in one of the labs at the University, after I helped him fix his ten-speed. I'd told him my plans for poor old Tom over a couple of beers. One of the killers wakes with a start at the feel of the needle, but his eyes glaze quickly and close again. The other hardly stirs, just moans a little. I'm not sure if the dose will be enough, so I take no chances, lash their hands to the bedposts with their ties, stuff their socks in their mouths.

I keep my knife sharp.

The Dragon Lady's tomcat has sprayed my bike again, but my bottle of dreams is empty.

Dawn on the prairie can be beautiful, even when the cold is sharpened at both ends. I pedal like hell and the day opens before me and all my hurts go numb.

Call me paranoid. But at least, if they come after me again, they'll have a reason.

The Food of Love

EVERYTHING HAS AN EDGE on it today. Like if you looked away it might still be there. Maybe it is just my blood in a bottle, cold, waiting for disaster. I always feel a little lighthearted after I give blood. Maybe that's why I go to see Silver. The noodles are just an excuse.

Spinach noodles today. He is feeding them through the cutter when I get there, gathering them up like a splurge of flatworms. When he has packaged enough to fill his orders, he drapes the rest over a maze of broomsticks to dry, turning his little house into a jungle. Sheila, he says, as if my name is enough.

Silver is the middle brother. As an only child, I have tried hard to understand the dynamics of larger families. I was outnumbered by my parents, without allies or enemies. If I ever have kids I will have lots.

The green noodles hang like kelp. Silver feeds the broad flat swatch of noodle into the gleaming jaws of the cutter. His turtle, Morgan, lumbers out from under the piano, nibbles a shard.

I thought I'd pick up some fresh fettuccini for supper, I say.

Special occasion? Hot date? We both laugh, even though it was Mickey who used to insist that noodles were aphrodisiac, and Mickey is dead. Mickey designed Silver's label, the one that says: IF NOODLES BE THE FOOD OF LOVE, DON'T OVERCOOK THEM!

Mickey was the younger brother, and his eyes never stopped laughing. I wonder, sometimes, if his eyes were laughing when he fell off that mountain. I sat down one day and tried to figure out how long it would take a person to fall a thousand feet. It's been years since I failed Mr. Doppler's Physics class, so I might have got it wrong, but it came out to something like eight seconds. I still can't decide if that's an awfully long time or a terribly short time.

No, I say. I just like your noodles. So does Morgan.

Spinach is her favourite. Tea?

Silver dances out of the jungle and fills the kettle. I try to pay attention to the details: each noodle swaying gently in its own pattern; the dying light on the leaves of the spider plant hanging over the sink; the way he stands poised over the teapot like a man engaged in magic, or a small boy making a peanut butter sandwich. I think sometimes of all the things I have lost through inattention. But maybe that is wrong. Everything is lost, anyway, but maybe if you pay attention you can at least know what you have lost.

How's Gordon?

He's okay, I say. Working too hard as usual. The new job isn't so demanding as the old one, so he has to work harder to find ways to make it stressful.

Silver laughs and pours the tea. Gordon is the older brother. I am married to him.

He's worried about your mother, I say.

She's probably worried about him, too.

The drugs don't seem to be helping. . . . Morgan lurches over and tastes my sock. Morgan was Laura's turtle. Laura left a lot behind.

Mother is an alcoholic, Silver says.

I don't—I mean—

No, he says. It took me a while to see it because I didn't want to. There she is, carrying on, keeping it all together, never missing a day's work, never losing control, never drunk, not so you'd notice. Through everything, Mickey's death, Dad's leaving. But I cleaned out her cupboards for her one day. She's got twice as many bags from the liquor store as from the grocery.

I know she drinks, but—

She is an alcoholic. I'm not saying that as some kind of judgement, for Christ's sake. I'm one too.

You? But you don't drink at all.

Now you know why. Alcohol is a solvent, you know. It dissolves lives.

Have you talked to her about it?

Why? If she wanted to know it, I wouldn't have to tell her. Anyway, she wouldn't understand me. She'd think I was trying to hurt her. Probably she'd be right. Maybe if Gordon talked to her . . . but he wouldn't.

Maybe you should talk to *him* about it.

No. I shouldn't even be talking to you about it.

Why not?

A waste of breath. Better I should be covering you with spinach fettuccini and Parmesan cheese. Let's go out and sail boats on my pond.

Silver has a fishpond in the backyard. Just a hole scooped out of the hardpan, full of murky seeping water and languid pond weeds, like spinach noodles hanging upward from the bottom. Two dozen ragged-finned oriental carp with deep unforgetful eyes, a gurgling inlet, a desultory overflow, splashing on slippery green stones. When he is not making noodles, or playing Bach (badly) on Laura's baby grand, or doing whatever else he does when time slows to a grind in his heart, he carves small sailing boats from cedar scraps, rigs them with string and pocket handkerchiefs, paints sad bright eyes on their bows and sails them. He and I have spent hours together at this.

This story has too many edges. However I try to handle it, it cuts. Gordon used to be fiercely jealous, in his silent, bonechewing way, when I laughed and rambled with Mickey. For some reason it never seems to occur to him to resent the quiet pleasures I share with Silver, his other brother. I have failed to understand the dynamics of families, but I think middle children are often unconsidered.

Mickey was a flame too bright. Silver says he flew off that mountain, would have kept flying, if the earth hadn't wanted him as much as everybody else. Gordon burns cold and secret and dangerous, like a fire moving underground. He can still burn me with a word, disarm me with a glance. But I tell him my small lies so routinely now that I believe them myself.

I come to Silver when I am cold. When the world has a hard edge, and cuts however I handle it. When my blood is still and waiting.

The big-eyed carp rise, ponderous, like thoughts from the unconscious, nose our boats as they limp across the dead waters, nursing a dying breeze.

I got a postcard from Dad, says Silver.

No kidding? From where?

Tierra del Fuego. Took three months to get here. They could be anywhere by now.

I'll have to tell Gordon. He hasn't heard a word.

Gordon once referred to their father as Hemingway with a hard-on. Gordon isn't a Hemingway fan, but Gordon is unforgiving. He hasn't forgiven their father for leaving, just as he hasn't forgiven Mickey for falling or flying off his mountain. Silver doesn't need to forgive, for he seems slow to blame. Though you'd think he'd have so much more to blame the old pirate for. What kind of father runs off to South America with his son's girlfriend? Laura left a lot, but no explanations.

Too many edges. Our lives get so tangled together, like a pot of noodles. Overcooked. I can see the beauty in a stark campsite, under the Southern Cross, in Tierra del Fuego. Even eight seconds of flight has an appeal. . . .

An edge on everything.

I invite Silver to come to dinner with us. He shakes his head and laughs. I hate noodles, he says, filling a plastic bag for me. If he asks me to stay, at this moment, I might never leave. He doesn't. I offer to pay for the noodles, knowing he'll refuse. I've given my pint today. Someone I don't even know, with Type O negative, waits in dread for the needle, the knife, a dribble of my life.

I leave Silver moving among his noodles, a graceless fish, swimming upside down. I go home to boil water and wait for Gordon.

———

It is raining in Tierra del Fuego. The Southern Cross is rained out. Hemingway hasn't had a hard-on since Punta Arenas, and tonight he overcooked the noodles. The sheep never shut up. There is straw in Laura's sleeping bag, and something else. Something alive. Hemingway is snoring.

Too many edges. Outnumbered.

Gordon jogs on his lunch hour. Like a fire underground. He can't run away from his doubts. He spends a lot on shoes. Likes to make love in the shower. Soapy Sheila. The suds of love. Down the drain.

Lives dissolving. Life is a solvent.

Gordon was a miserable baby. The squeaky wheel. Grease me! Silver at least let them sleep. Maybe they slept through his childhood? Anyway, it left little mark. Not like Gordon, who wet the bed 'til he was twelve, or Mickey, who burned a hole in the carpet the first time he laid his clever fingers on a matchbook. Caught in the middle, between a permanent stain and a scorch. Often unconsidered.

Details. So much lost. Everything lost.

Fresh fettuccini. Sheila smashes a clove of garlic and the kitchen swims. Gordon trying to lure her into the shower. Silver, eating a boiled egg, alone on the piano bench. A drying noodle pops and rattles to the floor.

Still outnumbered, though both of my parents are dead.

Richard's Secret

I WAS AFFRONTED WHEN MY BROTHER died. It wasn't supposed to be like that. He was the straight one, for God's sake. I hadn't seen him since Mom's funeral and now I was arranging his. I am three years older. We were close, once, I'm sure of it.

Time and geography came between us. I watched my life slip past, grabbed at fragments, caught a few: a wife, children, a degree, a lover, another degree, a job, another lover, a book contract. Another lover. Fragments.

Even my relationship with Brian, strong and safe as it feels, can't keep life from marching past my door and away, while I struggle to get my boots on.

Now this. A phone call to tell me the kid has died and left me everything. His will was scribbled on the back of a supermarket checkout tape and pinned beside the phone:

To whom etc.

When I die, I leave everything to my brother, William. Burn me—don't keep the ashes. I don't care what you do with them as long as they can no longer be identified.

William: Please format my hard drive.

Signed at the bottom, no date, but the receipt it was written on was dated last May. The doctor told me Richard had known about his heart condition for years.

———————

I flew out to Victoria. We had a small ceremony, and scattered Richard's ashes in the Gorge. The tide was coming in, so I guess most of him wound up in Portage Inlet, but maybe a little bit made it out to sea.

A couple of his neighbours from the condo came, and some of his work buddies. And Mila, his last girlfriend. I found her number pinned beside his phone and called her. She hadn't spoken to Richard for years, either, but she came. We had a drink, afterwards, on Richard's balcony.

Mila likes whiskey. She is a small, passionate, self-possessed young woman and I felt an odd anachronistic urge to flirt with her, seduce her. But Richard was hesitant on the turning tide, and Brian was in Toronto, waiting for my call.

I showed her the will. She smiled. That's Richard, she said. Too cheap to pay a notary fifteen bucks. I bet you'll do okay off him.

The condo's paid for, I said.

What do you make of this about the hard drive? she said.

He wants me to format it. Erase it.

Obviously. What's on it? Don't tell me you haven't had a look?

I don't know. He asked me to erase it. That seems to indicate he didn't want anybody to see it.

Sure he doesn't want *anybody* to see it. But maybe he wants *you* to see it. Don't tell me you're not curious. It's the only thing besides his ashes that he singled out. It must mean something.

I don't know. He didn't want it to fall into the hands of a stranger. He trusted me to destroy it.

But he didn't say you can't take a little peek first. Aren't you just dying?

I don't know.

She turned, drinking, looking out over the hesitant scum-fringed tide. Bluebeard's wives, she said, always used that key eventually.

When she was gone I poured myself another drink, and called Brian. We talked for almost an hour. I told him about the ceremony, even mentioned my odd attraction to Mila, knowing it would excite him. A small *frisson* of jealousy to keep some sort of edge on our passion. I mentioned the tide, but not the hard drive. When he hung up I refilled my glass and turned on Richard's computer.

The machine was a relic, an XT 286 clone, slow as gunk. I booted up, expecting to find the predictable household junk: accounts, letters, games, a mess of little-used software. To my astonishment I encountered a single word processing program, a good dictionary, and almost ten megabytes of text files. *Protected* text files.

Okay, Bluebeard, *now* you've got my attention.

I tried to break the code by chance or intuition, entering my name, Richard's birthdate, our parents' wedding date, divorce date etc. I entered everything I could think of which might somehow connect me to my brother: the name of a baseball player we both admired; the name of one we both hated. The name of our puppy that got run over, the schools we attended, anything. The machine was unimpressed. I thought we were close, once.

After some hours of this futility I threw up my hands, literally. No ambiguity was intended in Richard's message. He protected his secrets well and they would die with him. All that was left of my brother, the brother I might have been close to, maybe, if I'd given him a little more, if I'd dared to give him a little more, all that was left of Richard was on that hard disk, and if I wasn't to betray his trust, I must obey his instruction. All that was left of Richard. Not even dust.

I couldn't do it.

———

When the legal stuff was taken care of, I put the condo on the market, called Goodwill to get the furniture. I took Brian the Van Gogh prints and I kept the quilt my great-great-grandmother wove, that Richard got when Mother died. And I kept the computer. I took it home to Toronto and kept it, hard drive intact, in a suitcase under my desk.

I'd gone through everything, thinking he might have left a clue. But a secret code word is something you don't write down. For a long time I tried to think of what else he didn't write down. Nothing worked. Late at night, bored with my work, I would plug the old XT into my keyboard and bang my head against the brick wall that was Richard's legacy. I started to picture him, alone in that condo, picturing me, here in my study, yearning, now that he was gone, beating my brains out to know the secrets I never once asked him to share with me while he was alive.

This was his revenge. If he hadn't deliberately drawn my attention to the hard drive, I'd probably never have thought to try to gain access. The XT would have gone to Goodwill with the rest of the furniture. Protected as they were, Richard's secrets were safe anyway. He only chose to taunt me with them.

It even occurred to me that the locked files actually contained nothing, that Richard had created them simply to haunt me.

———

One weekend, Brian at a conference in Ottawa, one night, halfway through a fifth of tequila, I finally let go. *To hell with it. To hell with you and your mindfuck, Richard. You want me to format your hard drive, I'll format your fucking hard drive.*

Drunk as I was, I followed the procedure with deliberate care. The moment I struck that irrevocable key, reassuring the doubtful machine that yes (Y) I did wish to take this extremely drastic and arbitrary action, possibly erasing the work of years, the very moment I punched that (Y) I was in. I don't know how he'd done it, but somehow the combination of keystrokes which should have formatted the hard drive, instead unlocked every one of the protected files.

—————

Suddenly, I was sober. I filled my glass and drained it, but it didn't help. After months of frustration, I was faced with Richard's secret, confronted by it, and all of a sudden I wasn't so sure I really wanted to know.

I studied the directory and it frightened me. Hundreds of files, each apparently a chapter in a massive book: thousands of pages of single-spaced text.

Finally I filled my glass again, but I didn't drink. I selected the file named "Preface" and brought it up on the screen:

Preface

My name is Richard. Don't call me Dick. When I was born, the first thing they did was check to see if I had a penis. I did. (I repeat this check, daily.) Call *it* Dick, if you like.

Nothing much particularly exciting has ever happened to me (Richard). Many exciting things have happened to my penis (Dick). It *believes* they have, anyway. Being blind, deaf and dumb, Dick is incapable of distinguishing between real adventure and shameless fantasy. This is a most happy circumstance for a penis, or at least for one unfortunate enough to be attached to an introverted, marginally un-attractive and habitually boring person such as myself.

The adventures detailed in this journal, while containing not a shred of truth, nonetheless comprise an accurate autobiography of Richard's dick.

———————

I'd love to tell you it was wonderful. A work of genius. A quirky, erotic masterpiece, a roller-coaster ride of humour and passion and profound emotion, all brilliantly detailed from the point of view of a man's most sublime and ridiculous appendage.

It wasn't.

Well written enough, I guess. I read almost more of it than my heart could stand, simply because I found myself astonished by (and maybe a little envious of) my brother's direct yet evocative language. But when he described himself as habitually boring, he was right.

He quickly abandoned the anthropomorphic point of view and adopted a flat Caesarean third person. Each chapter might vary from the last in details of setting and atmosphere but was virtually identical in structure. Richard meets girl; girl is impressed; etc. Maybe the unremitting heterosexuality of the whole business caused me to lose interest more quickly than another reader might, but it could have been full of horny boys with tight cheeks instead of horny girls with big breasts and I am sure, in time, I'd have been yawning.

All addictions are boring. This is how they kill us: they bore us to death. But they do it slowly. I mean, I like a smoke but I don't stick the whole pack in my mouth at once and light up.

When the endless cycle of arousal and penetration and orgasm finally got the best of me, I went into the bathroom and threw up. Without noticing, I had finished the tequila, and next morning I felt as if I had been skull-fucked by horny porcupines. Brian came back from Ottawa and I wept in his arms.

And yet. I kept coming back to Richard's secret world. I stopped reading, really, but I skimmed, searching, I suppose, for something, anything, a single hint of relevance or character. Nope. Just fuck fuck fuck fuck fuck.

And yet. In time the thing did take on a curious power, transcending, perhaps, the limitations of the material. The rhythm of it took on a resonance which had nothing to do with the mundane, pornographic subject matter. This was sex, yes, but it was breath also—the endless cycle of death and rebirth. I didn't have a clue what had motivated my brother to record, on disk, every fantasy of his last years, (let alone what moved him to share this staggering collection with me, posthumously). But, eventually, I came to believe that Richard's legacy was a strangely powerful creation, possibly unique in world literature.

Brian found it a hoot. He laughed at me when I tried to express these thoughts, to analyze the work structurally, to search for patterns and allegories among the bodies. He liked to read bits of it aloud to me, out of context:

Hey, Bill, listen to this: *Richard pushed the bikini up and stroked her firm erect nipples. She tensed. "What if somebody comes?" she said. "No one will come," said Richard, "except you and me."*

It was Brian who found the letter. Brian has this habit of skipping ahead to read the ending of a book. I always feel this is a betrayal of trust, but he just laughs and says, How am I supposed to know if it's worth reading if I don't know how it ends? He even does this with mysteries, which always struck me as plain stupid. When he decided to see just where Richard had been going, he found it, an epilogue, tacked onto the end of the final chapter. The last chapter was indistinguishable from the hundreds proceeding it, except that it ended abruptly in mid-thrust. The epilogue was a letter to me:

William,

Since you are reading this you must have outlived me. Congratulations. I hope you haven't felt obliged to read the whole damn business. Even if you've only read a little, I probably owe you an apology. I'd like to offer an explanation as well, but who can explain himself?

Since I discovered, in early adolescence, the delightful gullibility of my penis, I have been shamelessly fond of fantasy. I don't know what possessed me to start writing it down, but when I did it enhanced the experience. For years, fearful of discovery, I burned each scribbled fantasy as soon as it had served its purpose. Only when I bought this computer did I begin this collection. A whim, maybe, or some futile attempt to hold onto the spent ecstasy? I don't know. But it wasn't until more recently, confronted by my own mortality, that I came up with the perverse idea of inflicting it on you.

The doctors tell me that one day soon my heart will kill me. Statistics tell me that only one percent of heart failures are brought on by sexual activity, but, what the hell, I'm going to go for it. Beats shovelling snow. I suppose they will have been too discrete to tell you that I was found with my prick still in my hand. But, if you've read any of this mess at all, I expect that is how you will remember me. I wonder did I have time to close this file?

No such thing as safe sex, William. I'm glad you have, so far, escaped the plague. I expect there is nothing in this book for you, and maybe that is why I have felt I can trust you with it.

Richard

p.s. I hope you can forgive me shutting you out of my life. As you can see, you weren't missing much. I hope you can also forgive me my misappropriation of the language you love. Maybe, if I have achieved nothing else, I've used more words to say less than any writer in history.

p.p.s. If you hit (N) instead of (Y), the formatting program will proceed.

Time and geography. Still got my brother's old computer, in a suitcase under my desk. We were close once.

No (Yes)

Maudie

MAUDIE DIED IN THE NIGHT. I like to think she died quietly, breathing out her soul in a delicate stream of bubbles, sinking one last time beneath the scuzzy waters of her pool. If she did suffer any death throes, only the elephants know. Ralph found her.

I found Ralph. He wasn't wringing his hands, but probably only because his mother never taught him how.

Ellen, he said. It's Maudie. She's dead.

Everybody loved Maudie. She'd been there forever, since the ark or evolution, whichever came first. She'd seen the elephants and the rhinos and the keepers come and go. Maudie loved her pool and her grub and didn't give a damn about anything else. She could yawn the scales off an acre of alligators.

Everybody loved Maudie, but Ralph had a special soft spot for her. Ralph is the new kid in the Elephant House. Out of school less than a year, still damp behind the textbooks, a little goofy but sweet. As for bright, well, he isn't about to put the sun out of business, but he can usually figure out which side of the bread has the butter, at least after he picks it up off the floor. He's a bit languid and overweight himself, so maybe he related more easily to Maudie's laidback hippo lifestyle than to the penetrating intelligence of the elephants or the unforgiving vigilance of the rhinos.

Ralph has a soft spot for me, too, which is harder to explain. I know he finds my cynicism intimidating, and my coarse language sticks in his craw. But I suppose I haven't been as mean to him as Walter and the others, and he appreciates it.

He was right. She was dead, all four and a half tons of her, dead at the bottom of her pool. We had to close the Elephant House most of the morning while we figured out how the hell to get her out.

First we drained the pool and put the slings and chains on her, then we filled it again to take some of her weight. We thought maybe we could winch her out with the Bobcat, but we couldn't get the machine through the door, and from outside we couldn't get any leverage at all. Walter, the head keeper, should have been wringing *his* hands, only he doesn't go in for that blood from a stone stuff. He contented himself with chewing our asses, as usual.

Finally we had to drain the pool again, and Walter sent Ralph for the chainsaw. The next part took hours. The saw went through poor Maudie's flesh and bones all right, but her leathery old hide kept shredding and jamming the chain. Ralph ran the saw and I loaded the pieces of Maudie into sacks and buckets and Steve and Kevin hauled them out and loaded them in the truck. By the time we were through Ralph and I both had bits of Maudie in our hair, our teeth, hanging off our eyelashes, dripping down inside our rubber boots. The elephants were depressed; the rhinos were livid. Even Walter looked grim, but maybe he was just feeling more than usually himself.

We started on her legs and worked our way up to her head. It took six washtubs just to hold her guts, and the stink got so terrible we were all adding our breakfast to the load. Except Ralph and Walter.

Ralph didn't get sick 'til it was all over. After we peeled off our bloody boots and slickers, I held his head for him and he held the toilet. Then we had a good cry and washed as much of Maudie off ourselves as we could.

Thanks, Ellen, he said. I didn't think I was going to get through that.

Shit, Ralph. When Walter kicks it, I get to run the saw. Let's go somewhere and get a drink.

Walter looked at us when we walked out in our street clothes, but he never said boo, so maybe he wasn't feeling himself after all.

———————

We went to the Armadillo and I ordered scotch and Ralph drank some nonsense with rum in it. The scotch didn't do anything for the taste of death in my mouth.

I think this is the worst day I've put in since the day my dad fell off the barn, said Ralph.

I didn't really want to hear about any days worse than this one, but it was obvious he wanted to talk about it.

It was the summer I turned sixteen, he said. We were fixing the roof. I don't know what happened, really. The doctor said he probably had a stroke, blacked out. I just looked up from driving a nail and he was falling. Never even yelled or anything, so the doctor must have been right. But I heard him hit the ground. All the way down the ladder I could see him jerking and twitching in the dirt. Like when you shoot a groundhog or a 'coon. I don't know how I got down that ladder.

Christ, Ralph. I want another drink. What about you?

Sure. You know, Ellen, I'm not sure I'm going to like working at the zoo as much as I thought.

Hell, Ralph. I've been here seven years and I've put in a few rough days, but this one takes the pizza.

The waitress took our order, didn't linger to chat. I guess we still smelled pretty powerful. After a couple more drinks it didn't make any sense to go back to work. The alcohol just made me tired, but it was having a different effect on Ralph. He started fondling my knees under the table, and leering at me, and suggesting we go somewhere, like how about my place? I knew he was fond of me, but I'm ten years older than he is and just because we had shared so intimately in the dismembering of an old friend, I didn't figure our relationship had to degenerate into bed. Besides, I live with my mother, so my place was out. Ralph didn't know I lived with my mother, but then my personal arrangements aren't any of his business.

What spooked me was when I realized that if I had another drink or two I was just as likely to say, What about his place? Just so I wouldn't have to go home and explain to Mom why I was off work in the middle of the day.

Look Ralphie, I said. You're sweet, but Thursday isn't my day to sleep with sloppy drunks. I'm real sorry about Maudie. I'm even sorry about your dad, but now I'm going to go home and stand under the shower for about an hour. Alone. See you tomorrow.

He looked crestfallen, so I leaned over and gave him a little kiss. I didn't mean anything by it; at least I didn't think I did.

Mom was sitting in the living room when I got home, watching *Donahue* and cleaning her gun. Since she finally hounded my father to his early urn, Mom is never far from her television, or her .357 magnum. She resents the fact that I go to work and leave her alone all day, though she doesn't seem to have any qualms about pocketing her widow's pension and living off my paycheque.

She lives in constant fear of rapists.

The gun belonged to my father. Neither of us knew he owned it 'til he was dead. I always suspected he bought it with suicide in mind, but I know Mom believes he was contemplating murder.

You're home early, she said. I suppose they finally came to their senses and fired you.

No. I came to mine and quit.

You'll never come to your senses, dear. Have you been drinking?

Yeah. It's not quite as cheap as hitting yourself on the head with a brick, but it's easier on the hair-do.

I wouldn't call that mess you carry around on your head a hair-do, dear. More like a hair-don't.

Thanks, Mom. Look, I'm pooped. I spent the morning packing nine thousand pounds of dismembered hippopotamus. I'm going to be in the shower for a long time, so if you need to use the john, do it now. Then I'm going to take a nap. Don't shoot yourself in the foot, okay? I've dealt with enough carnage for one day.

The shower is powerful and hot and I use lots of soap, but a sheen of death still clings.

I am tired and my bed is friendly, but I do not sleep. When I close my eyes I see pieces of Maudie. I try to think about other things, like what my mom would have said if I'd brought Ralph home and screwed him in my friendly bed while she was downstairs watching *Donahue*. Or why, seven years after Jake finally dumped me, I am still afraid to get involved with anybody else.

Sex, death, shit. You spend your life moving shit around, and trying to keep sex and death at bay, only some days you get it all over you.

I must have slept eventually, because when I woke it was dark and I had to go to the bathroom.

We had fish sticks and Caesar salad for dinner. I made the salad and Mom nuked the sticks. After dinner I washed up and she watched *Wheel of Fortune* and then we both watched *Jeopardy!* and I told Mom all the gory details about Maudie and she told me that in Africa hippo meat is valued for its delicate flavour and nutritional content. She saw that in some show on PBS. Finally she took her gun and went to bed.

I was sitting there, watching the room shrink down to darkness in the well of the TV screen, when the doorbell rang.

It was Ralph. I don't know who told him where I lived. If he'd stopped drinking since I left him it had only been to piss or catch his breath. He stood there, leaning against the door frame, a full moon grinning over his shoulder, a bottle of peach brandy in one hand and a rose in the other. He must have ripped off the rose from the yard next door; he'd scratched himself badly on the thorns and as he grinned and held it out to me a couple of drops of his blood fell on my white socks.

Christ, I said. What do *you* want?

Just wanted to 'pologize. Shouldn't have been so fresh. No call for it. No call at all.

I took the rose. That's okay, I said. But it's late and we've both got to work tomorrow.

No Maudie to feed, he mumbled. Poor Maudie.

Yes. Look, why don't you come in for a minute and I'll call you a cab.

You *do* forgive me, being so fresh, Ellen?

Sure. No problem.

Wonderful. Have a little drink?

No thanks. Here, come in and sit down while I call that cab.

No need, Ellen. I'm fine to drive.

The hell you are.

Sure. Only don't quite remember where I left my car. Hey. Should put that rose in some water.

Yeah. I'll do that.

He followed me into the kitchen.

Really nice place, Ellen, he said, embracing me ineptly from behind, so that I was not quite sure if he was trying to feel my breasts or just holding on to me to keep from falling over.

Thanks, I said, but you just finished apologizing for getting fresh earlier, so maybe you'd better go sit down in the living room.

Oops. Right you are. Wouldn't want Ellen mad at me. Nice place. Don't like the wallpaper, though.

What's wrong with the wallpaper?

Keeps moving around. Makes me not feel so good.

You're drunk.

Had a few. Memory of poor Maudie. Have a drink with me in memory of poor Maudie?

No thanks.

Okay. No call to get huffy. I'm going. Just got to use the little boys' room.

I showed him the john and he got sick. Once again I was there, holding his sweaty brow as he puked up booze and bile and saliva. He was a mess. He still stank of hippo guts, under the potent reek of puke and booze. I filled the sink and tried to clean him up a little, but he kept trying to kiss me with his vomit-spattered lips, and finally I shoved him out of the bathroom and ordered him to wait in the living room.

I put down the toilet seat and sat on it, took a couple of deep breaths. I thought about Maudie, dead at the bottom of her pool, about six washtubs full of her guts, about the keening whine of the saw as it fought through her skull. Then I got up, tightened the belt on my bathrobe and went to get rid of him.

He was passed out on the sofa, with his shoes on.

I actually picked up the phone to call a cab, but he looked so serene, sleeping there, and I felt so suddenly, ultimately weary, I couldn't face having to wake him and bundle him out the door.

To hell with it, I said. Sleep tight, Ralph. If you're still here in the morning, I'll drive you home.

I turned off all the lights but one, and went back to bed.

———

I don't know if I really slept at all. My whole life flushed before my eyes, like a plugged toilet. When I heard Ralph, downstairs, tripping over the furniture, I thought at first it was Maudie, returning to punish me for what we'd done to her.

Ralph didn't know I lived with my mother. My domestic arrangements were, after all, none of his business. I guess he was trying to come and get into bed with me. He got the wrong door.

I was galvanized. I lay rigid, awaiting the scream, the struggle, the deafening roar of the magnum.

No scream. No roar. Maybe I was dreaming. Maybe I've dreamed it all, but then why do I still taste poor Maudie's blood in my teeth? Eventually I found the strength to struggle out from under my blankets, wriggle back into my robe, put on my furry slippers and pad down the hall.

They were asleep; two fools in one bed. My mother had her arms around her pillow. Ralph had one arm around my mother, the other underneath him. Maybe he was reaching down to see if his prick was still there when the comfort of the sheets hit him like a freight and he passed out again.

These two deserve each other. But what do I deserve? Just to be on the safe side I got the gun out of the drawer in the bed table and took it downstairs, put it on the table beside the bottle. I tried a drink of the stuff, but it tasted like cough syrup cut with dead hippopotamus.

———————

When the doorbell rang again, I knew there was only one person in the world who could be ringing it. I've only ever known one person with timing like that. And I always knew he'd be back, someday, just when the last thing I needed was to see him there, insinuating himself back into my life like some slimy ghost.

It was Jake. The only man I ever really fell for. I never could resist giving the plugged toilet just one more flush, so I got up and let him in.

Seven years later and he looked like hell. Not just like he'd been sleeping in his clothes; Jake always slept in his clothes, when he slept at all. The fire was still in his eyes, but it had burned away all his beauty and left a scum of scar.

Full moon, baby, he said, as if, after seven years, that was all the explanation he needed. Maybe it was.

He was always skinny, but you didn't used to see all his bones. A couple of running sores on his chin.

Come in and have a drink, Jake. You look like shit.

Shit don't begin to describe it, babe. Shit has got a healthy glow to it, compared with me. Hey, give me a break. Ain't you got any real booze in the house?

Sorry. If I'd known you were coming I'd have robbed a liquor store.

You got the hardware here, anyway. He put down the bottle, picked up the magnum and pointed it between my eyes.

Don't fool around, Jake. That thing is loaded.

I should hope so. An unloaded gun is a dangerous thing to leave lying around. Might give somebody the wrong idea. Hey, you look terrific, kid. What's it been, five years?

Seven. Seven years. You might have dropped me a postcard.

Couldn't remember your post code. I heard about your old man. Too bad. I figured for sure you'd be married, a couple of kids hangin' off your tits. Hard to believe you're still eating shit out of the same bowl as the bitch queen.

I don't know, Jake. My mom is something of a relief after living with you.

Oh. Low blow. Don't bother to try chopping them off, babe, I sold them to buy drugs, years ago. But I am disappointed. I always knew I was going to make a hash of my life, but I kind of hoped I'd dumped you before it ate too deep.

Christ. If you came back to try and convince me that you broke my heart for my own good, it won't wash, Jake. I shared your grubby, flea-infested sleeping bag for almost two years, remember, and I've had seven years to think about it, and you know I'm damned if I can recall a single instance where Jake ever did anything for the benefit of anybody other than Jake.

That hurts, babe. But I won't argue with you. God knows I didn't come here to argue.

Why did you come, Jake?

That's what I keep asking myself. Shit, Ellen, I guess I've run to the end of my chain. But here I am, kid. Hardly a sight for sore eyes, but here in the flesh. Well, what's left of it. I guess there was something about you that stayed with me.

Christ, you really *have* hit rock bottom if you're pulling heavy shit like *that* on me.

Look death right in the eye someday and you may get a little serious for a minute, too, Ellen.

Don't talk to me about death, Jake. You want to know something about death?

Sure. Happens I'm kinda majoring in death these days.

So I told him. I told him about Maudie. I didn't spare him a single gory detail. Not the way we had to scoop her brains into the bucket with a shovel, or gather her infinite intestines into the tub with a manure fork, and finally with our hands. Not the shrieking of the saw through bone, reverberating in the concrete well of the hippo pool. I talked for a long time, and I cried again, and he held me, and it was like he was barely there. I could feel all his bones, could feel his breath, fluttering against his ribs like a squirrel in a cage.

Shit, he said, when I was through. Full moon, he said, and then neither of us spoke for a long time, and I knew by his silence that I had told him something.

I'm sorry, he said, finally. I shouldn't have come.

Maybe, I said. But since you did, and since I've got to go to work in a few hours, I'm going to venture an opinion. You know what I think? I think the thing about me that stayed with you was that I loved you. Don't ask me why. Not too bright, I guess. But shit, Jake, I really did.

You know, I think you did.

But you know something else? I loved Maudie, too. And that didn't make it any easier to do what we did today. Goodnight, Jake. Give me a call, sometime; you know the number.

He looked sad, and I had the urge to kiss him, but I didn't. I could still feel his bony arms around me, and I knew, suddenly, with devastating certainty, why he had come, what he'd meant to tell me. But all he said was,Goodnight, Ellen. And thanks.

Thanks for what? I said.

For Maudie.

When I walked by Mom's room on my way to bed, I could hear them breathing but I didn't look. I got into my friendly bed and a minute or two later I heard Jake let himself out.

And then I slept. Real empty resting sleep. My alarm woke me, just like another normal day. I got up somehow and peeked in on Mom. She was alone, sleeping with her arms around the pillow, like always. No sign of Ralph.

The bottle was still on the coffee table, but the gun was gone. It gave me a bad moment when I saw the empty spot on the table where it wasn't. But in the end I had to figure maybe that was the only gift I had left to give poor Jake.

Mom was still sleeping when I left for work. I cried a little in my car, but I was all right by the time I got to the Elephant House.

Ralph called in sick.

The Umbilical Trombone

THREE MONTHS AFTER it happened, John bought that damned trombone. It's not like we hadn't all suffered enough.

For me, the worst part was all the signs and pictures. I guess he was a good looking kid, and it made everybody feel good to keep reminding us. John said he hated it because it gave him hope, but I hated it because it reminded me how quickly I was learning to forget.

I wonder how *he* feels about it? Does he glory in it, does it even give him pause, to see, on every hoarding and lamp post, the face of the child he wanted, took, then threw away?

I never had any hope. Oh, sure, I had denial, but denial is when you know. I *knew*. It isn't a matter of belief. When you *know* it doesn't matter if you believe or not.

I tried to make John understand that, but he was too busy running away to realize he was leaving us behind.

———

. . . bright brass nestled in deep black velvet . . . finger in glove . . . the whole world turned and twisted in her golden bell . . . more beautiful . . . more deadly . . . dismembered in her case . . . than any assassin's weapon . . . taste the dust in the pawnshop window . . . stopped in to leave a poster . . . the broker's got

that startled rabbit look . . . want to throttle him . . . gives me a break on the price when he finds out . . .

He spent my washing machine money. He'd always wanted to play the trombone, but his mother disapproved. His father bought him a trumpet.

What could I say? I stood there with flour on my hands, watching him lovingly screw the bell and the slide together, there on the living room rug, and I knew it was over, that we'd lost him, as surely as we'd lost Nicholas.

If he'd brought home a bottle, I'd have reached for a glass. If he'd brought home another woman, I'd have forgiven them. He couldn't help but blame himself, but I couldn't blame him. I knew, always I knew, that he was cute but not to be trusted. And yet I left the boys in his care. I betrayed them, and *him*.

Only Nicholas no longer suffers from my betrayal. I know and it is my only comfort.

. . . he might be the one . . . the pawnbroker . . . perhaps he flinched to face me . . . felt the snap of Nicky's neck between his fingers as he fumbled over the receipt . . . run him through with a glance . . . skewer him with a bitter thought . . . no difference . . . no defence . . . read the psycho profiles . . . pass him in the street . . . peering from his dusty windows . . . stretched to a nightmare boil in the bell of polished brass . . .

And then it began. As if we were not all condemned to suffer enough.

We had to move. The neighbours were patient; we were famous for our loss; the help had poured in when we needed it, after John gave up his job to co-ordinate the search efforts full time. The community was kind; friends and family gathered close, filling the spaces all around us, leaving us nowhere to be alone together with our despair.

But now, the months pass and we are left with a thousand ghosts in shop windows, on lampposts, with the thousand corridors of the dream that all wake to the same nightmare, and the endless dirge of that damned trombone.

The dogs couldn't stand it. The neighbours were patient, but I couldn't stand their forbearance, or the howling of their damned dogs.

I rejoiced to leave the house I loved.

. . . when she sings I feel nothing . . . we are the dark throat of the music . . . nothing and everything fuse in our song . . . what comes out must once have been in . . . but it leaves us only emptier . . . with lips numb . . .

It is better here, though I hate how slow the clocks run, how eager each moment is to linger and bear the brunt of memory. The jets pass overhead at intervals. All the dogs are deaf.

He thinks I have no heart because I don't fart my grief into a brass bell, blurt it like a sick Bronx cheer to the ignorant world. He hates me because I have to live, because I still have Charlie, because I seem to be able to keep it all together.

I hate him because he is right.

. . . golden thread . . . so easily broken . . . hold on Nicky . . . feel nothing . . . all of us floating in this nothing . . . only a fragile thread . . . a single strand of golden song . . . don't let . . .

———

I had to do it for Charlie. He's had his childhood crushed like a bug, but surely he deserves a chance to grow his own scars. When I found John teaching him how to hold the instrument, how to blow through a kiss tight as a banker's asshole, I put my foot down. He was always cute, never could be trusted.

The trombone has to go, John, I said.

He looked at me. I think it was the first time we'd made eye contact in months.

If it goes, he said, I go with it.

I know that, I said.

———

. . . deep as a well . . . my songs bubble up from inside . . . pass him in every street . . . a thousand times a day I throttle a stranger in the vain hope he may be guilty . . . all the dogs in my new neighbourhood . . . are dead . . .

———

I wish, I wish, I wonder. The other street people live in awe of him. Life closes over us all. I buy Charlie a violin, but he has brass bells in his eyes and I know I have lost him, too.

———

. . . bubbles up from . . . every street . . . a thousand strangers . . . the thread is fragile . . . a single doubt will slice it like a wire . . . every note . . . every tear

. . . bubbles up from inside . . . seeing him always . . . the man in the sweater . . . the man in the van . . . his face looks more familiar all the time . . .

I have no pictures of Nicholas in the trailer. I do have one picture of John. Charlie cut it out of the paper, one of those local colour shots in the Sunday supplement. It shows him standing under the bridge, his overcoat too big, his hat too small, and showing the soil and soot of every stoop and dumpster he's lately called home. The damned trombone shows a few dents, and not much shine, but he blows his brains out in silence now, magnetically askew on the refrigerator door.

. . . the taste of brass is bitter on my breath . . . the thread is broken . . . forgive me, Grace . . . I knew not what I did . . . to you . . . the faceless one wears my face now . . . Nicky screams his terror as I pass . . . on every street . . .

Hitchcock Diary

THIS MORNING, DRIVING TO WORK, sitting at the red light at Tattersall and Quadra, you check your mirror and Alfred Hitchcock is driving the Dodge behind you. It's an old gold Dodge, mid-seventies, rusty, with the broken grill, and he has something indistinct and bulky in the back seat. A bass fiddle, maybe, or a body.

The light changes, you drive on up the hill and he turns south. Just one of those famous cameo appearances? But why here, why now? What is he doing in your life? You thought the man was dead.

Okay, it's only been a week since she left you. Maybe you're not quite yourself, yet. But you always saw your life as more of an Antonioni flick than Hitchcock.

Everything is different, like there's this hot wire wrapped tight around it, keeping it upright and rigid and awake. But nothing has changed. Every day is an offprint of the last. The painters are on the job, now, and the day is full of fumes and radio noise. You're somewhere else, thinking: *Maybe it makes sense, maybe your life really is a Hitchcock movie, has been all along. Not one of the classics, maybe, but marked by his style: the ominous signals, the introduction of characters by their feet, the overwhelming significance of objects, a ring, a lighter. A television set?*

There is an edge but you are not sure if you have already fallen.

The drive home is unremarkable, no dead directors in the rearview. You open a beer, kick your boots off, turn on the TV. Nothing changes. Everything different. *All you ever do is sit there, she* said, *drinking beer, smoking spliffs, clicking. We have no friends, we never go out, not anymore, we never do anything.* And on and on, all true. You flip through the channels; nothing on but you keep flipping. *I work hard,* you told her. *I'm not pushing a desk, you know.* Blah blah blah. You keep flipping. Tampons, beer, cars, more beer, more cars.

Something strange happens. It is difficult to explain. It's like suddenly you're watching yourself from somewhere very far away through the wrong end of a telescope. You watch yourself set the remote on the table and press the red button. You watch yourself watch the light implode, the colours swallowed by the dark.

And then, just as suddenly, you're no longer far away. You are right inside, and it is so sudden, so terrifying, right here, side by each with this rising, swelling anger, and then you hear this little crack, like a knuckle cracking, only you know it is your mind.

You pick up the television set and yank the cable right out of the wall. You stand for an instant, the set heavy in your arms, and then you fling it through the picture window.

Double glazing explodes out into the darkness. You feel very centered and whole and human. Kind of an overwhelming rush of wonderful ordinary. Then you hear the screaming.

The woman is bleeding from several cuts to her face and arms, caused by the falling glass, but she is screaming because your television set has just killed her boyfriend.

Oops.

Time is so slow you swim in it, a strong current. The hugeness looms but you decide to deal with *that* later.

The damp sucking darkness of late October at the gaping frame. The chill right to your heart and your kidneys. You start to piss yourself. You grab it and make it to the bathroom. Stand, watching the stream encircle the bowl, thinking: *I can't believe I just fucking killed some poor guy and I'm standing here watching myself piss.* But on some whole other level your mind is turning over, a cold engine, grinding. And time is a tide, slow as mud; you watch the seconds develop and mature and pass away and you're calculating. *If somebody has phoned the cops already, and there is a car in the neighbourhood, your goose is cooked. But the combined odds are in your favour. Either way you've got to have two minutes. Plenty of time. Be thorough. You've just destroyed your life and it's fight or flight time and you're out of here. But stay calm. A couple of minutes, still, they have to finish their donuts, dust the sugar off their uniforms, plenty of time, as long as you pay attention, don't waste it, time is a friend, obliging, creeping slower and slower, a glacier now, moving in increments immeasurable by the naked eye. Be thorough, cover the trail. Wallet, photographs, letters, clean out the desk, tear the page out of the phone book, still a minute left, at least, probably much more, don't panic, shit, the kitchen drawer, the photo of you with her that her sister Karen took. The night sucking all the warmth from the room, don't look, you don't have to look, if you look it will be too late, time will be the enemy, no need to look, that single glimpse will stay forever, clear, don't think about that, not yet, take your toothbrush? God knows where you'll be sleeping tonight. Clean shirt? Drugs? No, time is slow enough, don't want to drown in it. Or maybe. Maybe for later, when you can't say later any more. Enough, your minute is squandered.* The night sucks.

Your truck is parked in the lot at the back. You lock the door of the apartment, thinking: *They'll kick the door in, there goes the damage deposit,* and then you remember the window and you laugh, and then you remember the guy on the sidewalk and you stop laughing. No one in the hall. Press the elevator button then take the stairs. *Don't run. Walk smoothly, like you've been doing it all your life, like it's the most natural thing in the world, don't listen to the pounding of blood in your ears, just keep breathing, keep walking, the most natural thing, down the stairs, out the back door, across the lot, braced for the shot, but calm, right, just a guy, going somewhere, no sirens, no cops with guns. Turn the key. Starts like a dream. Good thing you blew a day's pay on that new battery, after all. Now let's get the fuck out of here.*

Pass the cops at the corner of Harriet Road. They don't even see you. They aren't looking for a live guy in a pickup truck, not yet. They are still looking for a dead guy on a sidewalk.

You wind up at the bar at the Ingraham Hotel, ordering a double whiskey and wondering (now that you seem to have jump-started time, again) just what the hell you're going to do after you've finished drinking it.

Remorse would be appropriate, but even the double whiskey can't convince fear to loose its hold on the emotional mother-board. *Think. Time is vapour, now, evanescent, this must be what they mean by the mists of time. The whiskey drying you from the inside and time subliming into the ozone and even as you hug the bar and watch the bartender blend margaritas and wonder, the cops are consulting, commencing their investigations, the neighbours will be helpful, the car-insurance computer will spit out your driver's license photo, the plates on the truck. Have to ditch it. But they'll watch the bus station, the airport, the ferries. Have to lay low for a bit, but where? Jesus Christ, you never meant to hurt anybody. You don't know what happened. You just lost it for a minute and now that guy is dead and you're fucked. Turn yourself in? Throw yourself on the mercy of the court? It was an accident, your honour. I'd lost something, a lighter, a key, a ring? I thought it might have rolled under the television and I was lifting it to have a look when something startled me, what, I don't know, a cockroach, a cockroach as big as a rat and wearing boxing gloves. I lost my balance, your honour, I staggered, I stumbled, the weight of the television getting away from me, tried to hold on, your honour, to bring it down, keep it in the park, but it was going, going . . .*

Get hold of yourself. Plenty of time to go to pieces, later, when you are safe. But where? They'll check hotels, campgrounds. You need somewhere, someone.

You get quarters from the bartender, but you don't know who to call. You want to phone *her*, but you wonder if there are enough quarters in the world to reopen that line.

The page from the phone book is still in your hip pocket. You pull it out, smooth it out. You look at it while time is exploding, taking you with it, flying away in all directions at once, seeking a place of safety, knowing all the time that the fat man is behind the camera now, for sure, and safety is only a concept.

You let a quarter drop.

Hello.

Hi, Karen.

Who is this?

I have to get in touch with her.

Oh, you. She told me you might call.

You've seen her.

She called me. Are you all right? You sound strange.

Yes. No. I don't think I'll ever be all right again, actually. Listen, I've got to talk to her.

She's gone. Back east. She made me promise I wouldn't give you the number. Sorry.

What else did she say?

She said you didn't need her, you had cable.

I don't have cable any more.

Congratulations. Hey, man, you'll get over it. People break up all the time. Look at me. I've been dumped so often, they've got my name on one of those bins out at the recycling yard.

It's not that. I've done something really stupid.

This is supposed to surprise me?

There's this guy. He's dead.

He's what? Jesus, where are you calling from? It sounds like a bar. It *is* a bar.

I wondered why you were calling me. You're drunk.

No. But I have to get out of here before I am or they'll get me for sure.

Who'll get you? This isn't some kind of—

Listen. We've had our problems, Karen, I know that. But I never meant to hurt her and I never meant to hurt that guy and now if you can't help me I am really and truly fucked.

What guy? Is there some kind of a fight going on there?

It's just the hockey game on the TV. Listen, can I just come over and talk to you for a few minutes?

Jesus. I've got to stop answering my phone. What the fuck is the point of an answering machine if you can't screen out calls from psychos? I'll put the coffee on.

You walk past the truck without looking at it, but when you are sure they haven't staked it out you go back and get the multi-driver out of your toolbox and switch your plates with the Toyota beside you. Twice you have to crouch down and hide while guys stagger or shuffle to their vehicles, but neither of them owns the Toyota. You lock the truck and put your keys in the briefcase with the rest of your hastily gathered life, pitch it in the hotel dumpster.

As you wait to cross Douglas an ambulance screams by, but you know it is too late for the guy on the sidewalk, way too late; one glimpse out the shattered window was enough to know that. Better to send a street cleaner. Shit.

It's a long walk to Karen's place in View Royal, keeping to the back streets, stretching it out, time outstripping you, stride for stride, adrenalin puffing to keep up. It's drizzling.

By the time you get there you're soaked and you're starting to have to think about it, around the edges of your mind. You're wondering what you will say but she's heard a report on the radio, put a couple of two's together and come up with a number too huge for her calculator. Glass and coffee everywhere.

Look what you made me do, you stupid son-of-a-bitch, she says, but she lets you in.

Time has dissolved, finally, a solar wind of random particles, singing in the spaces where your molecules bond.

You tell her everything, even the Hitchcock thing, but you can hear your own voice, your own words, and you know they are senseless.

You have to turn yourself in, she says. If you don't call the cops right now, I will.

You're right, you say, but you can't seem to get the phone in focus; one second it is right there in front of you and the next moment it is flying away, into the next room, the next house, Colwood and beyond, beyond your reach if your arm were a million miles long.

Maybe you've never taken responsibility for anything in your life, she says, but you aren't going to be able to duck this one. You blew it big time, this time.

It was an accident. I never meant . . .

What *did* you mean?

I don't know. It was symbolic. A gesture.

Some gesture. What about the guy on the sidewalk? What's *he* symbolic of?

I don't know. But shit, *his* troubles are over. I mean, we all have to die, don't we? The guy wasn't young, maybe he had cancer. Maybe I saved him from a horrible slow death. I mean he sure as hell never knew what hit him.

Yeah. You did him a favour. I can't believe I'm sitting here listening to this.

———————

You can't believe she is still there listening to you babble prevarications and debate determinism with yourself (talking fast so as not to let yourself think) hours later when the spot comes on the radio:

. . . the name of the victim has not been released, but sources indicate that he was well known to police and the matter is being treated as gang or drug related . . .

Hear that? you cry. I iced some thug.

Get hold of yourself. You sound just like the television you threw out the window.

But don't you get it? I'm *really* fucked. No one will ever believe it's an accident. And even if the cops don't put me away, the thug's thug friends will.

She looks at you for a long time, and then she says, You'd better get out of town.

It is the first time she's said anything other than how you'd better turn yourself in. The moment she says it you know she is going to sleep with you.

It turns out you're not the first criminal in her life. She knew this guy, back in Hamilton, a hustler, a small-time dealer with ambitions. Now he's a respectable business man, at least to the naked eye, but he knows people, he might help you, he might not, she hasn't seen him in years, but it is all she can offer you, and definitely more than you deserve.

She cuts your hair off. When she stands in front of you to inspect her handiwork, you reach for her and pull her toward you, bury your face in her bosom. She doesn't stab you with the scissors.

Every time you push it in you see a dazzling explosion of glass, but every time you pull it out you get blood and brains on exposed aggregate. Even so, by morning, you know you've been sleeping with the wrong sister all your life.

———————

You ride the Esquimalt and Nanaimo Railway north, walk onto the ferry at Departure Bay. The haircut, the earring, the beret, a simple disguise, but you wear it confidently because without it you are naked and doomed. You ride the trains east, looking at feet, knowing you are got, you are caught in the tunnel, but sure.

You tried to destroy the monster, but it gotcha. More fool you; monsters can't be killed by mere fools, that's what makes them monsters, and us fools. You've been swallowed by the angry ghost of your television; your life will be an endless chase scene, punctuated, perhaps, by beer and cars and tampons but the end will be inevitable and violent and trite. Where's the master's hand in all of this, anyway?

Hamilton will help you, build you a new identity, a new persona, a new career. You will become an assassin, employed by men you will never meet, erasing their enemies from the planet in your own chosen way, with a rain of well-aimed appliances.

You will live high and fast, for a while, drinking whiskey so rare and old it has to be delivered by armoured car; sleeping with women who have no self-respect at all. *So high, so fast, no time even yet to think about it, really think about it, about. It.*

Until the final contract comes, of course. *What could a woman like her have done to earn the enmity of men so cruel?*

The Warden

THE WORST THING wasn't finding him, hanging by his belt from the rusty hook where the crofters used to hang their hams to cure. The worst thing was the first thought, after the shock, the blue glazing fire that burnt the tongue of thought: After this, no one will blame me if I crack that bottle.

It was him, the Canadian kid, the polite one, the one who shook my hand and asked me my name when I took his hostel card and his money. I can't remember the last one of them who bothered to ask me my name. I'm just "The Warden" to them. But then, they don't go and hang themselves in the drying room.

I didn't open the bottle, not then. But I did take it out of the cupboard and set it on the table and sit down in front of it. The bottle I bought one day when I just couldn't make it by the off-license one more time and see the amber glow in the window there like the answer to something. But when I got home with it she looked at me with that infinitely sad but resigned look of hers, that I-knew-you-would-but-I-hoped-you-wouldn't-but-I-knew-you-would-only-I-really-did-hope-maybe-this-time-you-wouldn't look, that made me want to pitch the damn bottle in the river. Like that was the answer to anything. Instead I set it in the cupboard and told her it was my talisman, my proof to myself that I didn't need the bloody stuff any more. Because if I could resist it there on my own shelf then I would know I was really free.

A bloody lie, of course. I could live fifty years and never crack that bottle and it would still be grinning at me, that lovely death's head grin, telling me I'm fooling myself. There is no victory. My triumph is empty. Because when I walk into the drying room to check if the sheet sleeping bags are dry, and find a gentle young Canadian hanging from the rafter with his eyes bugged out and his face gone the colour of mouldy cheese and all his beauty gone, my first thought, after the shock subsides and my guts stop strangling my breath and I can think at all, my first clear coherent thought is of that bottle.

And were I to drink it, or give it away, or pour it down the WC, the thought would still be there, virgin and amber and glowing on some shelf, like an answer to everything.

I didn't open it. Not then. The thought was bad enough. But I knew I was lost, just like that young Canadian. I sat and looked at the morning sunlight, lost in the depths of that good single malt. I wondered about him, that young Canadian. Oh, yes, I'd cut him down, loosened the belt around his neck, but he was oh so cold and there was nothing more I could do. I'd called the constable, down in the village, but he was out on a break-in call, not expected back for an hour or so.

I left that bottle unopened and went to my desk, got out his hostel card, looked at the photo, so young, so serious. I opened the card and looked through the stamps. He'd been on the road a long time; he had stamps from a dozen countries in Europe, from Spain to Hungary. Some wardens stamp the cards when they come in, but I do it in the morning, when the person checks out, so I hadn't added my own stamp. I got out my inkpad and did it now. There was nothing else I could do for him.

Was there a message in that firm handshake, that asking me my name? Maybe if I had just opened myself up a little, given just a little more than my hand and my name and change for a fiver? Maybe if I had asked him where he'd been, where he was going,

Christ, asked him into my kitchen and poured some of that good Scotch down him, let him share the loneliness of his road. . . .

I don't know. I am a traveller, myself, though my road is different now. I've hiked and hitched and cycled in my time, bedded in strange hostels (and when did I ask the warden's name?) or alone with a bottle of cheap wine under a hedgerow. My road is different now. I camp here under brooding skies with a woman who binds me with a tyranny of kindness and love and I let the world flow over me, pass through me. My road leads through the souls of my fellow human beings.

I take their cards and their money, cook them breakfast if they wish. I send them off with my stamp and a smile, and few of them ask me my name, and few return. They come from everywhere, Americans, Australians, Japanese, Finns, once a couple from Mongolia. They stay a night or three; they move on.

I grow my garden, milk my cow. My wife has her sheep and her rabbits. We travel through the lives of the people who use our many beds, but we don't touch them. We are on a fast express; we dare not lean out too far and try to touch, lest a part of us be carried away. By what? By whatever it is that carries *them*, the wanderers?

Only one has come to stay. And we sent his ashes and his hostel card back to his mother in Canada. . . .

Set me up another. . . .

The Eureka Effect

THE FIDDLE SLEEPS in its nest of silk. The rollerskates are silent, and do not dream. The fiddler sleeps fitfully, tense as a fiddle string, unable to fill the broad bed, missing his warmth, his solidity. The rollerskater breathes slowly in his narrow bed.

Between the layers of the bitter night, Randy pitches his tent. Steam heat ticks in the walls, an insect clock. Beyond is the cold that kills. It is the hour when dreams poke fingers into the waking mind, prying loose the word and the vision. Randy knows this hour. His body cries for bed, for the comfort of her body which fits his own like today snuggles up against tomorrow. But here, in the space between, his mind will pitch camp, the blank page will stare into the pit of his futility, and he will wait for the effect.

The car slides through a tunnel it makes in the night, the headlights blunt against the blowing snow. How could you just stand there? she says, the wheel biting into the palms of her hands. How could you, how could you just stand there and let her say those things to me?

What things?

Oh, Christ. Don't pretend you don't know what I'm talking about. Every time it's the same.

Yes, he says. You make sure it's going to be the same. You set yourself up. You don't give anybody a fucking chance.

Who? Who don't I give a chance? Your mother? Your sister? What fucking chance have *they* ever given me?

You set yourself up.

Of course. It must be my own fault. God forbid anybody in *your* family could be anything but perfect.

That's not fair. You're over-reacting. You always over-react. I don't even know what you're so freaked out about.

Of course not.

Do we have to go through it again?

Go through what?

The same goddamn thing.

It is not the same thing. You really don't have a clue, do you? You want me to just shut up and be sweet. Be a fucking ostrich, man. *Live* in your hole. Pull the fucking pages in over your head.

That's it, isn't it? You're so damned resentful of my work. It always comes down to the same thing.

It has nothing to do with your fucking work. If you would pay a little attention to somebody besides yourself. . . .

Selina. This is crazy. I'm sorry.

What good is that?

No good at all, I guess.

I don't know. *You* tell *me*.

Forget it.

In the back seat, Chris and his plastic robots fight a silent battle. Lasers which kill silently, like the night, like the cold.

Sometimes the old man has the radio and the TV going at the same time. Anything to push out the silence where she no longer sings. The barn is fine, the sweet chewing of the cows, the warm shit smells, they fill his life as always, a quiet continuity. But the house roars with angry silence.

———————

When the cold bears down, merciless and mean; when winter stretches well past the ends of the night and bites the nose off tomorrow morning; when midnight turns the screws of memory and drives a wedge between a man and his hopes; when words run dry and the breath of ultimate futility frosts the windows; when night reaches beyond all horizons and we kill the ones we love with words like double-edged razor blades. . . .

———————

Please, please, please, just go, just leave me alone, just shut up, I just don't want to hear it again. . . .

———————

The car needs shocks and every frost heave is a nail in the coffin of conversation. The cold is clean-edged and unmoved; the night opens just enough to let us pass and clamps tight behind.

When I think of the things I've given up for you, she says. The chances we never took because you were too scared to risk it. The shit I put myself through, the shit I put *Chris* through, for you.

Her hands burn through the wheel, but the road never veers. You've worn me out, she says, you and your fucking lump-on-a-log passivity. I've had to push and strive, to dig every little bit of commitment out of you; I've had to pay attention every moment, watch every detail, sorting through the garbage for crumbs to keep us going, while you, you sit there, your coffee cup freezing to your hand, your boot heels wearing a dent in the top of your desk, waiting for light, for a bolt of lightning, for your goddamned Eureka Effect.

Just go, she says. Just leave us. No, you won't even do that. I'll have to be the one to leave, just like I've had to always be the one. You were right. It *is* always the same.

The blank page perishes at the first stroke of the pen. The night bleeds light. Every quarrel sinks in time into the muck of compromise, the comforting compassion of need. Waiting to suck us under.

Her fiddle sleeps, wrapped in its own magic. Her fingers sleep, knowing the notes, even in sleep. His manuscripts are awake, babbling to each other in their cardboard boxes. Unread. His fingers dance with the pen across the empty floor of the page, dance to a music that bursts through the dreamwall, screaming. . . .

What do you want me to say?

What you really feel.

I don't know any more. I try to say what I feel, but you just twist it to mean something else.

Okay. Blame me.

I'm not blaming you. It's nobody's fault.

Bullshit.

Meaning what? That it's *my* fault?

I didn't say that.

It's what you meant.

Don't tell me what I mean.

Jesus . . .

We dance on our own guts with spike heels. The words don't matter; incidents are irrelevant. The feeling is enough, killing and silent as the winter, crunching down. Chris, in the back seat, silent, piling up the bricks of a fragile fantasy, knowing, if he can just hold his breath long enough, we will not drown.

But the cold is so pure, so clean, killing thought, murdering trust and betrayal, stripping messy living flesh from the perfect bones of beauty.

We met in the dance. Light whirled from our bodies like sweat. The fiddle wept in her hands and freed me from my net.

The joggers are all frozen into their sweatsocks tonight.

Waiting. Randy waits for light. His coffee cup leaves a stain on the blank page. Squeezing out the tears. Blood from the bone. Failure haunts his heels like a starving dog. Kick me again. Randy has given too much to his art to succeed at life; his happiness lies shattered in shards of killing conversation, a dropped cup. He has given too much to his life to succeed at art. He has dreams but they will not stick to the page.

Can't win if you don't buy a ticket. But that last buck hurts like hell when you rip it from your flesh. The pen is a blunt instrument.

The old man hates the ghost images, the ghost voices, full of false cheer, vapid platitude, but he fears the silence more. A cup of strong tea, cooled with fresh milk, sweetened with syrup, rattling against the saucer like rain.

He resents his feelings, so trite, so predictable. He has laughed at the blade of colder winters, shaken his fist at drought and locust storms. But she was there.

He turns off the television, turns its vacant stare to face the wall. He unplugs the radio and opening the kitchen door he hurls it into the unflinching night. He slams the door, bolts it hopelessly against cold, against death. Pours her a cup, strong and pure, the way she likes it.

The wheel is cold as bone in her hands. The highway falls away before and beyond, like a mind balanced on the brink of sleep. Chris, in the front seat beside her, is serious but determined.

Where are we going, Mom?

Away. Just away. Far away.

Can we go to Mexico?

Mexico might be far enough. Somewhere away from this cold.

Okay. *That's* decided then. How far is it to Mexico? Is it warm enough there we can go swimming?

Sure, honey.

Oh shit, Mom. I didn't pack my swim suit.

The highway is a tattered ribbon of drifting snow and frost heaves. In the back seat the fiddle dreams in its nest of songs, and every bump reminds it of the dance. In the front seat, Chris fingers the silent wheels of his battered skates.

A very blunt instrument, with which to beat out one's own brains.

The Eureka Effect. The interface between layers of consciousness.

The hole in the wall of waking where dreams ooze through. The light which hides.

The sane, the sensible, the hardworking, all are sleeping now, dreaming to forget. The dangerous wait in shabby rooms. For the effect. Lives shattering around them.

Leave it lie, Randy. Come to bed and let me forgive you with my body, forgive you everything you can't forgive yourself. Let it lie and warm me. Flesh is everything, while it lives. Beyond is winter, and the rest. Leave it lie.

Don't cry, Mom. He'll be okay. We'll send him a postcard when we get to Mexico, so he'll know we're fine.

The television stares hard at the wall. The radio sleeps in a snowdrift. Her tea grows cold.

A blunt instrument. A stain on the page. The first stroke. . . .

The feeble thrust of the headlights cringes so gradually that they are almost hurtling in darkness before they miss the light. And then not hurtling. The darkness thickens and chokes the engine as it swallows the light. Selina's foot drives the pedal toward the floor, but the car does not respond. The headlights fade to a puddle of cold grim light and the engine turns over once more and gasps to silence.

The last of the dashboard glow fades like a dying firefly, 'til darkness is complete. Alternator? Fan belt? Tools in the trunk, flashlight dead with cold. Wind like a fist. Trunk frozen shut. Fingers turning to popsicles. Turn the key, one sad grind, then a click.

Chris's voice, serious, but not scared: What do we do now, Mom?

We wait.

Waiting. For morning. For spring. For rescue. For light, oozing through. For the wind to be silent. For everything to be silent.

For the effect. The interface where life and death grind together. Where Celsius and Fahrenheit intersect, the fragile heat of bodies cannot long sustain the insatiable night. Wrapped together in a single blanket, the fiddler and the rollerskater shiver and wait and try not to listen to the wind.

I wish Randy would come and fix the car, Mom.

So do I, honey.

She'll be back. She always comes back to me. Our lives are intertwined like the roots of grasses. We are sod. So why this hollow in my guts? Why does love have so many layers, the strong which cannot be bent by any hand, and the weak which undermine?

Randy pitches camp between the layers of love. Between the weak and the strong.

I don't want to talk about it. You don't even try to understand. You're not stupid, but you are a fool, Randy. The little things just wear me out. I try and try, but I get so I just can't see the point. The whole stupid business with your keys. The scenes with your family. The way you arrange your own failure, and then wallow in it. I just can't take any more, can't you see?

She'll come back. She always comes back. The layers of our lives are fused. Why is there this well inside?

Steel and glass resist the wind, deny the snow, but cold is in the car, stealing.

My toes hurt, Mom.

Here, take your shoes and socks off and put your feet inside my jacket.

I can't. My laces are in a knot. My fingers don't work, Mom.

Here, let me. Damn it, Chris, why are your laces always either undone or in a knot?

I don't think I want to go to Mexico, Mom. I want to go home.

Randy wants to go home, too. To strike camp, say to hell with it. The wind is a vise, tightening on night.

Come to bed. Forget. Let the walls fall.

A stain on the page.

First the pain, and then the place where pain falls through the wall. Hypothermia. The voices dull to a mumble.

My feet are going away, Mom.

Even when we were easy together, there was a hard edge. We muddled through, but it was never enough for you, Selina. You demanded clarity, precision, accuracy. My life isn't like that. I strive for vision; I bank on revelation, but I was born on a foggy Friday. If it ain't one thing, it's another.

I give you the clarity of cold, the precision of winter, the accuracy of death. I have no one but the two of you, my lover, my child, yet I drive you to the edge, over the edge; I feel the night closing on you. I scream in the silence of my heart, but I cannot save you from the trap I have laid, hoping only to catch a bit of myself.

We wait. For the effect. For clarity, cold as tonight.

The old man sees it first out of the corner of his eye, like something not quite remembered. A light beyond the window, a fire on the horizon. He leaves the teapot to grow cold. He pulls reluctant life into the guts of his snowmobile and fights across the wind toward the highway.

He finds them: a woman clutching a fiddle, a small boy hugging a pair of roller skates, their backs to the wind, laughing and warming their hands and feet and faces in the glow of the brightly burning Toyota.

Hydroponics

STACY WAS CYCLING HOME from class when a scared kid in a black Maverick ran a red light, turned her fifteen-hundred-dollar mountain bike into a twisted little pile of garbage and put her in a chair for the rest of her life. The kid had just been flashed by a couple of city cops; he had four ounces of very smelly hydroponic skunk under the front seat and he panicked. He said he never saw her 'til he hit her.

I've known Stacy since she was a squealer, and she was. A wild child, she drove her poor mother up the wall, climbing trees, jumping off the porch roof, shrieking like a banshee in the sheer delight of childhood.

Her father was a good cop, but he was a drunk. Her mother was well-meaning but not very strong. The kid in the Maverick finished them both off, but he hardly slowed Stacy down. John killed himself within a year. He chose his favorite poison. The only reason it took that long to kill him was the tolerance he'd built.

Marge had never been strong, and she went to pieces. Less than two years after becoming a cripple, Stacy was an orphan. Kevin Preston, the kid in the black Maverick, hanged himself in his cell. I don't know what became of *his* parents, but I don't have a good feeling about it.

Stacy hung in and completed her degree, with honours, in botanical science. She bounced back like the athlete she is. Got a nice ground floor apartment, with a ramp, grew orchids and hydroponic celery in her living room. She found a job at the Experimental Farm, put her money in the bank, bought a VCR and a compact disc player.

———————

When the idea first started bouncing around Narcotics, I thought of Stacy, but I never said anything. Nothing came of it that first time, but a few months later it was back, this time from above, and I'd just heard that cutbacks had hit the Experimental Farm and Stacy was looking for work.

The idea was simple enough. Most of the marijuana showing up in town lately was local, grown indoors, often hydroponic. Our plan was to open our own retail outlet for hydroponic and indoor gardening supplies and equipment. Then all we'd have to do was monitor our own customers.

The time seemed ripe. Most of the local growers were bringing in equipment from the mainland, or picking stuff up piecemeal, here and there. One guy did open a shop here a few months back, and he did good business, too, 'til we busted him with forty clones in the crawlspace.

Let me get this straight, Stacy said to me, wheeling away from her window boxes and locking my eyes. You want me to be a narc?

I want you to help stop the people who are putting the stuff on the street that put you in that wheelchair.

I wasn't put here by a *plant*, Lance. Plants don't run red lights. I was put here by a stupid kid running from your stupid law.

We sat in silence. I'd always admired the way she called a spade a spade.

———————

A month later, *she* called *me*.

Hi, Lance. How's Narcotics?

Habit forming, I said. You find a job, kid?

Nothing. Actually, Lance, that's why I called. . . .

———————

We called it Hydroponic World, and the place was an immediate success. Stacy knew her stuff; she researched her market, even offered free weekend seminars on getting started in soil-less gardening. We gave her free rein in running the business, and she gave us copies of her files.

It stunk. In her unguarded moments, I could see she hated me for doing it to her, hated herself for letting me. And mostly, hated herself for liking it. Because she was a natural. She had the analytical mind of a trained scientist, but she also still had the intuitions of the wild child who knows she really *can* fly.

Within a month of her opening, she had identified a dozen growers. Some of them were totally open with her, trusting her kindness and obvious vulnerability, confiding that they were stocking up on necessities quickly, before the heat caught on to her existence and staked out her front door. That one got a good chuckle around the station.

Larry wanted to bust the lot of them, clean up and get out. The Chief was in favour of a selective harvest, knocking them off one by one, trying not to kill the golden goose. Larry thought that was stupid, risking the whole operation just to make ourselves a nuisance.

I agreed with him. But I wasn't about to see the considerable investment of department money, not to mention Stacy's hard work, blown to bust a dozen amateur growers. I argued for sitting tight.

In six months, I said, we might have enough fish in the net to make some kind of a difference. Meanwhile, Stacy is doing enough business to cover our overhead, so why sweat it?

They bought it. Narcotics is habit-forming, like I said.

Stacy was relieved when I told her we were letting her first crop go to seed, and she didn't try to hide it. I knew she'd been steeling herself for that first bust. I appreciated her candor more than ever, now that I knew how good a liar she could be. And she *was* good. Not one of those growers had a clue. Not one of them could see in her anything more dangerous than a broken flower child. But I knew.

What I didn't know was that she was already falling in love with one of them.

His name was Stephen Barbarian, an easterner of Armenian extraction, but he was living under the alias Strider Jacks. He had two priors for cultivating, back in Ontario. He was old enough to be her uncle. I don't say her father, because I knew her father well, and like I said, he was a good cop, never took a bribe while he was sober. No unreformed greybeard hippie could ever have been her father, not if he was old as Methuselah.

This Barbarian was no ignorant weed farmer. He'd earned an honours degree in political science from Queen's, back in the sixties, but I guess he kept that sheepskin to clean buds and roll spliffs on, because he never used it for anything else.

I'd been afraid for Stacy from the day she opened, afraid she'd blow her cover, afraid the pressure would get to her, afraid, mostly, that she would come to hate me for luring her into the fascinating degradation of undercover work. But I guess I never saw where she was most vulnerable. She seemed so self-contained, so independent, never for one moment allowing her grief and loneliness to show. Maybe if I'd been able to offer her comfort instead of work. . . .

She was taken with Barbarian. Why not? He was tall, strong, probably good looking, though how you could tell under all that shaggy hair and behind all those bushy whiskers is beyond me. But he was smooth. He'd talked a judge in Ontario out of sending him to jail, though he'd been caught red-handed with over a thousand plants in full bud, ten grand in cash, and a .45 under his pillow.

As for his age, I'd known for a long time she was impatient with the self-centred men of her own generation.

They shared an interest in books. Stacy hadn't been much of a reader before her accident, but stuck in that chair she had become an addict. The first time Barbarian came into the store he found her reading Mayakovsky, and after that he never came without bringing her a volume or two from his extensive personal library.

Her passion for literature had come to rival her passion for horticulture, but both those passions took to the back seat the first time Barbarian touched her hand and told her how beautiful she was.

Do I blame myself? Of course I do. I'd never had the courage to tell her.

He was married. The two boys who lived upstairs in his house were his wife's children by a previous marriage. She worked downtown as a legal secretary. His wife was there in the bed beside him, when we kicked the door in.

Stacy'd had him stuck in with her list of "Possibles," but he jumped straight onto the "Definite" list when we ran a check on him. She'd been trying to shield him from the first time he came in, but he had too much hair to escape our notice. When I told her we'd put him on the "Definite" list she shrugged, spun her chair away.

I don't know, she said. Unless he's getting the bulk of his supplies somewhere else, he hasn't got much of a crop going. Maybe he's changed. He's got a family now.

She was good, but I'd known her too long not to hear it.

We got a warrant that afternoon.

I'm good, too, but she'd known me too long not to know. I wasn't even back in my car before she was on the phone to Barbarian. I don't have to imagine that conversation; I've listened to the tape a thousand times. I don't know if she knew we'd put a tap on her home phone, but if she did she didn't care. She knew I knew, anyway.

Strider? It's Stacy.

Hi, kid. What's the matter?

Get rid of it, Strider. They know who you are.

Baby, they haven't got a *clue* who I am.

No, listen, this is serious. They'll send you to prison. What about your kids?

Hey, relax girl. You're spinning your wheels. I'm small potatoes. Why should they bust *me*?

Because I as good as asked them not to.

What?

Listen, Strider, there's something I have to tell you. If you never speak to me again, that's cool, but you have to listen to me now. The bust is coming and it's coming down on you. I've been working for them all along, don't you understand?

His laughter was deep, warm, rolling. Even when he recovered enough to speak that dark laughter kept bubbling up, lifting the lid.

You had me going for a second there, Stace. We've run this tape before. *The cops are watching the place. There are hidden cameras. There are rumours the big one is coming down.* Baby, when you've been nurturing the delicate herb as long as I have, you come to understand that the worst enemy of the herbalist isn't the Heat, it's the Fear.

Jesus Christ, you asshole. Don't you understand English? I'm a *narc*. You think it was easy for me to call and tell you that? You think I'd lie about something like that?

All I know is you've been trying to talk me out of this crop since I first walked in and caught you reading *The Bedbug*.

I was trying to fucking warn you. Maybe if you weren't so stoned you might be able to take a hint.

Maybe if I were a little more stoned you might be able to make me believe you. But I doubt it. I can imagine you almost anywhere, Stacy, doing almost anything. You're a remarkable and complicated person. I can see you running for Parliament, or writing the Great Canadian Novel. I can see you lying around stark naked in my bed, preferably some weekend when Sylvie and the boys are over on the mainland. The one thing I can't picture, Stacy, is Stacy, the narc. Nice try, honey. It's the thought that counts, but I'm afraid you're a lousy liar.

The whole place smelled of skunk. It was a warm night and Barbarian and his wife were in bed in the front bedroom, naked under a cotton sheet. When he reached under the pillow for his gun, I shot him.

As the Chief said, we were lucky the poor bastard wasn't black or a Sikh or something, we'd have had a riot on our hands. But I admit it didn't look good, and the press had a field day.

I shot him when he went for his gun. I *knew* he was reaching for his gun. I don't know if I even had time consciously to remember the .45 they found under the pillow when they nailed him near North Bay. I saw his hand and I knew that if I hesitated one of us was going to die anyway, and it might be me.

Maybe Stacy was right. Maybe he *had* changed. When I shot him through the heart he was reaching for his watch.

Larry backed me all the way. He'd been right behind me and he swore that the flash of my flashlight beam on the crystal of that Rolex was just like the glint off the nickel-plated barrel of a weapon and if I hadn't pulled the trigger he was just about to. Myself, I tend to believe that if Barbarian *had* had a gun, and I hadn't shot him, he'd have drilled us both, got up and put his pants on before poor Larry recovered from his surprise enough to remember that thing in his hand was a gun. But I appreciated him backing me up.

Still, it didn't look good, especially when we found only fifteen plants in the basement. I got put on the shelf 'til the Board cleared me. The Chief pulled some strings and got Stacy her old job back at the Experimental Farm. The Hydroponic World project was a bust, and I had to take full responsibility for that.

––––––––––

It must have been six months later, she called me out of the blue, at home. I hadn't seen her since it happened, hadn't spoken with her, though I did drive by her place now and then, to see that her windows were still green. She said she wanted to see me.

When I walked in and saw the bottle of Bushmills on the table it gave me a shock. That was John's drink.

You haven't called me, she said.

I guess I figured you were pretty mad at me.

Why? Because you murdered my lover? I guess I was pissed off at you for a while. I'm over it. Drink?

She'd started without me. The bottle was half empty, but she wasn't drunk. Her eyes were very clear, her face just a little flushed. The top two buttons of her blouse were undone and she wasn't wearing a bra.

I'm sorry about what happened, Stacy.

She filled two glasses half full of whiskey. No ice, no water, no soda. Just like her old man used to drink it, straight. Do me a favour, Lance. Don't fucking apologize anymore, okay? It spoils the mood. She pushed the cleaner of the two glasses toward me. Maybe she *was* drunk. I'm not a drinker. I'll take a glass of wine with a meal, a cold beer on a hot afternoon, that's about it. I tasted the whiskey, winced as she took a healthy swallow.

It wasn't like . . . I started to say, but I caught the sudden impatience in her eyes and realized I was still apologizing. Whatever she wanted from me, it wasn't excuses.

Sit down, man. Take your boots off. We got catching up to do.

You're right. I like the way you've done your hair.

He was a dangerous character, you know, she said. Did you know that all the clothes he wore were woven from pure hemp? The man was a fanatic, all right. Sylvie and the kids, too. He sent those kids off to school every day in duds made out of a plant so dangerous that just growing it in your basement makes people kick your door down in the middle of the night and shoot you in your bed. They were lucky the other kids didn't try and smoke them.

Maybe I better come back when you sober up a little.

Fuck that, Lance. You can't wait that long. I had a case of this shit delivered yesterday.

Jesus, Stacy.

Relax, Lance. We don't have to drink it all tonight. Besides, I want to talk to you.

That shit killed your father, Stacy.

Nonsense. It just kept him looking alive for years after he was already dead. You knew him a long time, didn't you, Lance?

Fifteen, sixteen years, I guess. He was a good cop.

A good cop. I wish I could picture that. *His police skills were excellent. He could inflict maximum pain and leave no mark. He could win the confidence of the innocent, prove them guilty to themselves. . . .*

Everyone knew he had a drinking problem, Stacy.

Wrong again, Lance. Everyone *thought* he had a drinking problem. Daddy didn't have a drinking problem, Lance. That was his *cover.* I'm surprised it fooled a professional like you. You saw through *my* secret in a moment. Didn't it ever occur to you to wonder why I changed my mind? About your little "proposal"?

Yeah. I wondered. I've never seen through you, Stacy, not for a second.

Your insight was always selective, Lance. That's what happens when you fall in love with someone.

I blushed. I don't think I'd blushed in twenty years and it felt so weird and embarrassing that it made me blush harder. My ears steamed. Her clear eyes never left my face, and I hid behind the glass of whiskey. By the time I came out from behind it I'd drunk more than I'd meant to.

You're good, Lance. Or shy, or both. I never even suspected. I knew you loved my father, but I always thought underneath you must hate me for what I did to him.

What *you* did to *him*?

I mean, why else would you come to me with such a plan? Everyone else in my life was treating me like some poor wilting princess, expecting me to write angst-filled poetry, or maybe become a spokesperson for the rights of the handicapped, to hold my head up and give courage to others. Not you. You saw through me that far. You took one look at me and said: *She'd make a good narc.* I had to respect you for seeing that.

I should never have involved you in. . . .

I don't know. I think it was sweet. There was Stacy, a prisoner to the suffocating awkward kindness of everyone in her life, and you held out a hand to her, like you were saying: *Hey, kid, you don't belong up there on that wheeled pedestal. Get on down here and root around on your belly in the slime with the rest of us. It's where you belong.* . . .

I'm sorry, Stacy, I never. . . .

Oops, the man's starting to apologize again. Drink some more of this shit and listen to me, Lance. I thought you were offering me some kind of redemption. Don't move your fucking glass while I'm trying to pour! Now listen, this is important, I thought you hated me because you knew, that you'd seen through me all along, like you were telling me I would always be living a double life, but maybe if I went with it, maybe if I immersed myself in betrayal so deep I couldn't ever trust anybody again, most specially not myself, maybe somehow, some way I could understand what it was about me that I'd always had to betray the only ones who really loved me.

She started to cry when she said that. I wasn't blushing any more, though she was leaning toward me as she spoke and I could see both her nipples.

I felt grey and sick. The whiskey was beginning to strip the layers of pretense from my personality and I didn't like it. I felt suddenly that if I didn't get a breath of fresh air soon I was going to throw up, but I didn't move.

She put her empty glass on the table, turned away, rolled over toward the window, cranked it open. Getting stuffy in here, she said. The air from the window tasted of barbecuing hamburgers and carried distant undecipherable syllables of conversation. Out there, the neighbours were carrying on like it was a normal, ordinary, Saturday afternoon.

My stomach settled a little, although I had to fight the urge to ask her to shut the window.

She wheeled back to the table, reaching for the bottle, but I got it first, moved it out of her reach. She looked me in the eye.

Taking charge, Lance?

If I have to, I will.

I know. That's why I called you. That and because I felt I owed you.

Owed me?

Shit, Lance, I did it to you, too, didn't I? I blew the project, probably your career. I grew up in the lap of the department, Lance, I know how these things go. You'd have been running Narcotics in a couple of years if I hadn't come along and fucked things up for you.

None of it is your fault, Stacy.

Of course it is. If I hadn't gone soft for Strider you wouldn't have had to kill him. That was the part I just couldn't figure out. Why'd you have to kill him? I mean I knew as soon as you knew that you'd have to bust him. I was compromising the whole project. But shooting him kind of blew the whole project out of the water, anyway. Then I realized you were in love with me; you'd been in love with me all along. You had to kill him.

It wasn't like that. I thought he had a gun. . . .

Yeah, I know. And I really truly never imagined he might be married when I let him put his hand in my panties. Ha, you're blushing again. You're wishing maybe you'd pumped a couple more rounds into him, aren't you? Right in the guts maybe, or even lower. That's what I like about you, Lance. When you have to take charge, you take charge.

You're drunk. You don't know what you're saying.

Better pour me another. Maybe you can get me drunk enough to forget I ever said it.

She pushed her glass toward me, leaning forward again. To avoid staring I tried to concentrate on splashing a little whiskey into her glass. She picked it up, looked at it critically, looked at me critically, said, Only good advice my daddy ever gave me, he said: *Never let a man buy you a drink if you don't want to cook him breakfast.* You like eggs, Lance?

That's never been what I wanted from you, Stacy.

What *do* you want from me, Lance?

I don't know. Maybe all I want is for you to know I never meant you any harm.

I can't *forgive* you, Lance. I never *blamed* you. You did what you had to do. Can I believe you will never willfully hurt me again?

Yes, I said.

You got handcuffs in your car, Lance?

Sure.

Go get them.

I started to say something else but her eyes silenced me. I got the cuffs from my car. When I came back she had refilled both our glasses, but she wasn't drinking.

Why should I ever trust you, Lance? You're a narc, a professional; double-crossing is your bottom line. Give me those.

She opens both cuffs, hands me back the key, cuffs her right wrist to the chair.

Skill testing question, Lance. If you were the one cuffed forever to the chair, and I were the one with the key, the badge, the gun and the penis, would you ever be able to trust me? Don't answer right away; think about it.

I thought about it. I guess not, I said, finally.

Wrong again, Lance. You'd *have* to trust me. You wouldn't have very much fucking choice, now, would you? When the other guy holds all the cards it's a little late to start asking to look at the deck.

What did your father do to you, Stacy?

She rattled the handcuffs and said, Don't tell me you recognize his style, Lance?

That son-of-a . . .

Hey. That son-of-a-bitch was a better man than you'll ever be. He knew when to take charge. He never hurt me. He loved me and needed me and I betrayed him.

You didn't betray . . . I started to say, but then she tore the next two buttons off her blouse, dropped them, one in her drink, one in mine.

You don't know a thing about it, she said.

I know you aren't responsible for . . .

Her breasts were pale and perfect, her nipples staring at me, daring me not to stare back. She interrupted me again: Have you still got the same gun?

What?

The gun you killed him with.

I . . . well . . . yes.

Let me see it.

I don't think that's . . .

Let me see it, Lance.

I took out my .38, placed it well out of her reach, on the table.

What's the matter? she said. Don't you trust me?

I . . .

You don't, do you? Sorry, Lance, trust has got to be a two-way street.

Something huge and inappropriate was happening in my trousers. I pushed the gun across the table toward her. Did I imagine that I saw her nipples stiffen as she reached to take it?

You're an idiot, she said, pointing the gun into my eyes. I knew

I was going to die, then, the bullet crashing into my face with the blunt force of a sledgehammer, a single instantaneous impact of sufficient force to blow all memory of fear and lust and betrayal forever out the back end of the beyond.

She was right; I *was* an idiot.

When I opened my eyes she was still pointing the gun at me, but not at my face.

Drop 'em, she said. The hand holding the gun was steady, her clear eyes were dead sober. Me, I felt like I'd just drunk the whole case; the undertow was stripping the sand from under my heels. I fumbled with my belt but I saw a tic of impatience in the corner of her mouth and my full pockets hit the floor with a thump. She said nothing, and her expression never changed, but she indicated my briefs with a circular motion of the .38.

Stacy. You're drunk.

Yes, she said, straightening her arm, sighting down the barrel. I'm drunk but that's only my cover, Lance. It doesn't give you the right to try and rape me.

What the . . .

You must have been a little drunk, too, though, Lance, to be careless enough to let me get hold of your gun. Or maybe that's what you really wanted from the start. To give me a chance to betray you, too. Is that it, Lance? Is that what you really want from me?

I don't exactly remember what I said, but I guess I was wrong again, because she shot me.

The Broom

THEY WALK BESIDE THE HIGHWAY. The man walks in front, the woman behind. They walk with the careful, unhurried steps of people who remember many miles, and know many more stretch ahead.

The pickup truck slows just a little. The three white people in the cab have probably been drinking; certainly they are laughing. The white boy in the back of the truck is drunk and drowsing, but he rouses himself when the others rap on the glass. He braces himself and gets his hands around the handle of the dirty curling broom which lies among the tools and empty bottles.

The man senses it coming. He turns in time to see the woman struck down, sent reeling to the ditch with a blow from the broom.

The people in the pickup are shrieking with laughter as he kneels beside her and stops her blood with his shirt.

This is the hardest moment. All the warmth in the world, pressed between bodies in bed. Two hands in one glove. Small hairs mingle, seals in the sun; skin smooth pressed close to skin, a dry perfect kiss, sealed in the weight of sleep; all the warmth, no room for cold, folded around each other, one glove, smooth; seals in the kiss. . . .

The hardest moment. Cal pulls himself from the bed, from her arms, extracts himself like a tooth. She rolls over and sighs and gathers what is left of his warmth closer around herself and he shivers and shovels himself into his work clothes.

Cal turns on the bathroom light, shuffles in the half-dark of the kitchen, trying not to wake her. The darkness is unyielding beyond the windows; the coffee is loud in the pot.

She wakes for his goodbye kiss. All of him returns to her except his steel-shanked boots. Her kiss is as warm as all night long and if his boots weren't pulling on his feet he might fall back into it.

See you tonight, honey.

The morning bites, but the darkness is cracking. Jupiter pierces the solid blue of the east.

The work is hard, but Cal's body responds willingly to the spade, the wheelbarrow. He is free in his mind to think of her, rising from the diminished warmth of their bed, wriggling into her red gown, boiling an egg, washing his smell from herself in the kitchen sink. Drinking tea and reading as dawn comes crashing in at the window. Pedaling away to her first class.

The mud clings to Cal's boots, his spade, his gloves, his clothes, cold and ugly, but he is patient and stronger every day. The earth yields. Dawn comes up, harsh and bright, but the sun's glare doesn't penetrate to the basement below the gymnasium, where Cal and Kevin are digging the sump. They have been working in this hole for days, weeks, an eternity of gumbo. Inside his boots, Cal's feet feel like clods of mud, slowly hardening to stone.

Several times each day the water in the hole gets too deep and Cal and Kevin lower the heavy pump and suck out the muck. They take turns digging in the hole and loading the sticky clay into the wheelbarrow, wheeling it on planks to the hoist, loading it into the box, climbing up the ladder, hoisting it up and piling it outside to freeze in the February cold.

Kevin keeps up a running commentary: Fucking hole; fucking wheelbarrow; fucking mud; fucking shovel; fucking hoist; fucking hell; fucking hole. . . .

By lunchtime the sun feels almost warm. Cal would like to sit in the sunshine and eat his sandwich, his apple, but his feet need the warmth of the gas burner in the company shack, so he crowds in with the rest of the crew.

Saw a hitchhiker this morning. Couldn't fucking believe it, says Grant.

Should've run him down, says Kevin. Should've broomed him. Kevin swigs Koolaid and gnaws a fingernail to the quick. Shit, he says, I always keep an old curling broom in the back of my truck. Go out on the weekend, broom the fucking Indians. One time my brother hit this squaw so fucking hard the fucking handle snapped right off in his hands.

Holy shit, says Bill. Must've felt that one, eh?

Should've seen that cunt take the ditch. Christ it was funny. Made my brother buy me a new fucking broom.

Cal's sandwich tastes of mud.

The afternoon wears thin. Cal attacks the mud with the blade of his spade. Should've said something. How could I sit there and just. . . . Should've told them. What? That they make me puke? That they are stupid assholes? Hey, Kevin, how'd you like to feel what my shovel handle feels like across the back of your head? See how *you* like the taste of mud.

Cal fights the earth; somehow the day is chopped into spadefuls and piled to freeze. The pump sucks.

––––––––––

What's wrong, honey?

Nothing.

Bullshit. You've been in a mood ever since you got home.

Just a lousy day in that lousy hole.

You been digging that damn hole for weeks now, but most days you come home with a smile for me.

It's just those assholes I work with. They just get to me after a while.

Kevin the prick?

He's the worst. The rest are just as bad. What bugs me is I just sit there and don't say anything.

So say something.

What? They already think I'm strange. Not that I give a shit what they think. But nothing I say would make any difference.

Shit no. But it might make you feel better. What can they do? Fire you? Tell them to shove their hole.

I'd like to.

The world is full of assholes, Cal. Let's go get some ice cream.

All the way to the ice cream parlour and back, Cal walks between her and the street. Chopped into spadefuls.

Piled to freeze.

––––––––––

Friday. Payday.

Hey, Cal. Stop for a quick one with me and Kevin?
No thanks, Grant. I got to get home.
Suit yourself.

———————

Funny bastard, that Cal.

Damn good labourer. Best fucking labourer we've hired since we hired you, Kevin. Not easy to find a guy that comes to work these days. Not for what *we* pay, anyway.

I'll drink to that. But he ain't very fucking friendly, is he? We been in that fucking hole seems like fucking weeks and he ain't said more than: Here, that's enough in the fucking wheelbarrow. Don't know what his fucking problem is.

I got an idea, actually.

Yeah?

I drove by him and his girlfriend up on Broadway a few days back. Pocahontas.

No shit?

Honest injun.

Looker?

Not bad, for a squaw.

Shit, Grant. A piece of tail is a piece of tail, I guess, but I wish I'd've been in the back of your truck. I'd've broomed the both of them. Have another?

———————

Cal has always been a quiet one. When his mother used to say, Penny for your thoughts, Cal? Cal wouldn't deal. But now, as the sump eats deeper, his mood darkens. Each lunch and coffee he broods behind his lunchbox, chewing on his own powerlessness.

When he puts away his spade at the end of each day, he feels the imprint of the broom on his palms.

————

For God's sake, Cal. If you won't talk to me about it. . . .

I'm sorry, honey.

It's me, isn't it? They've found out you're living with an Indian and they're giving you a hard time.

No. It's nothing to do with you.

Bullshit. I've known you long enough to know when you're lying. I've had it, Cal. I've had it up to here with trying to cheer you up. And you won't even talk about it.

There's nothing to talk about.

My Friday class is cancelled. I'm going to hitch out to the reserve, visit my sister for a few days.

————

The bed is broad and cold as tundra. Permafrost in the boxsprings. Cal is weary in every bone and sinew, but his visions will not let him sleep. He sees her, beside the highway, blood on her face, her eyes glazing slowly.

She doesn't return. A penny for your thoughts, Cal.

Should've said something. . . . How could I just. . . .

————

Still taste the mud.

Baseboards

I DON'T THINK MUCH ABOUT IT, Loris, he said. I guess if the only thing I'm here on this planet for is to show you a bit of a good time, that's plenty, ain't it?

Donnie drives a bread truck. He loves me like a puppy loves an old shoe. Some days I *feel* like an old shoe.

I've been at the hotel twelve years next month. One of my boys is starting junior high next year, but I'm still one of Mrs. Windsor's *girls*. People I know wonder how I stand it: making the same beds; cleaning the same toilets; day after day, always a smile for the bitchy customer. But every day is different, full of glimpses into the passing lives of strangers. I'd never steal from a customer, even if I didn't know it could mean my job. I've known some who did, but they couldn't last, it ate them up. I *do* spy, relentlessly. There's no harm in it. They are strangers, foreigners sometimes, and it's not like I root through their underthings or read diaries or anything. I just take note of the casual clues: the book on the bed table, the wine bottle in the waste basket, the dirty magazine stuffed behind the curtain. I draw my own conclusions.

The carpenters were a bit of a nuisance, but it broke the monotony, and the new baseboards sure made vacuuming easier. The guy that did Three was always polite to me, and to the customers. With the long hair and the little beard he looked kind of like Jesus in coveralls. He had this strange name, Lenis, but then who am I to talk? Loris is actually short for Dolores. I couldn't stand the name Dolores. I wondered if Lenis was short for something *he* couldn't stand, but I didn't ask.

On his breaks he'd sit in the room where he was working, eat fruit and yogurt, read. He was always careful; he'd put a newspaper on the chair, another in his lap so he didn't spill yogurt on the rug. He'd usually read these novels, library books by people I'd never heard of. One day he was reading this magazine with pictures of vegetables on the cover. I asked him if it was a gardening magazine. I know a bit about gardening; I guess I thought we might get up a bit of conversation. He seemed nice, but a little shy. When I said that he just laughed this odd laugh.

Later, when I came back with clean towels, he was out in the hall at his saw. I sneaked a look at that magazine. It turned out to be this review magazine, all about art and books and there were more pictures of vegetables inside illustrating this short story. I thought for a minute what a coincidence it was that I'd never met anybody named Lenis before, and here was another one who wrote short stories about vegetables. Then I made the connection and understood why he laughed like that.

He was taking his lunch break when I stopped in to tell him that 309 had finally checked out. I apologized for my mistake about the magazine. He laughed again.

A gardening magazine would probably pay better, he said.

I always thought it would be fun to be a writer, I said, still mostly just trying to make conversation.

Me too, he said.

Isn't it?

Let me ask you something, Loris. Don't you ever wonder just what the hell is going on here? What possible reason there might be?

For what?

Never mind.

I felt sorry for him then, for all he didn't know, and I sure couldn't tell him. To change the subject, I said:

Do you write stories about anything besides vegetables?

Sometimes.

Where do you get your ideas?

I steal them.

You're kidding.

Ideas are cheap. Even good ones are quite inexpensive. It's twisting them 'til they crack open and spill the feelings inside, *that's* the tricky part.

I wouldn't know where to start.

You can start anywhere. Where you start isn't any more import-ant than where you wind up. You can pick up on anything. A face in the street suggests a character; a character suggests a situation. Or vice versa. Doesn't matter. You could write a story about an encounter in a hotel room between a carpenter and a chamber-maid. As far as that goes, I probably will.

About you and me?

Not really. What's to say about us? A couple of ordinary working folks get a few miles of baseboards on and all the beds made up without coming to blows? What you want to do is take ordinary and twist it. Apply a little torsional stress and see what gives. You and I might *suggest* the characters and the situation, but to make a story out of it, as opposed to a *novel*, say, you'd want to strip away the inessentials, make archetypes of us, then twist a little more, shatter that fragile skeleton with a glimpse of emotion. Of course it helps if you throw in something to build dramatic tension.

Like what?

Doesn't matter. Sex is good, I guess, but it's kind of obvious. Maybe the suspicion of sex; maybe a jealous husband, mistaking a spiritual or even an intellectual connection for something phys-ical, reacting with inevitable violence.

My Donnie wouldn't hurt a fly.

This is fiction, sweetheart; stay with the program. How about this? The carpenter is also a writer, not a famous one, but he *has* sold a few stories to little magazines. The chambermaid sees his name in one of the magazines; she's interested in writing; she strikes up a conversation.

I thought you said this was fiction.

Bear with me. The possibilities are numerous. You could even get a little postmodern, whatever the hell *that* is supposed to mean. You could introduce a self-referential element, write a story about a carpenter and a chambermaid, discussing how to write a story about a carpenter and a chambermaid. You could call it "Baseboards." One word titles have a certain brute force, especially when they're grounded in the physical. Brevity is a blunt object.

Sounds like a pretty blunt story to me, actually.

You're right. Sex and violence is probably a safer bet. Or at least the suspicion of sex and the suggestion of violence.

You mean like they could talk about writing stories and get all postmodern and blunt, but her jealous husband thinks they are up to no good and the carpenter writer never gets to finish the baseboards on Three?

You're getting the idea. You could even have the writer slash carpenter write a story about the encounter. The old story-within-the-story motif. What the hell—always steal the best. Only in his story he maybe suggests things that didn't exactly happen, and when the story gets published it somehow falls into the hands of her jealous, but fictional, husband. He doesn't understand about poetic license and one morning the fictional equivalent of Mrs. Windsor gets her archetypical knickers in a knot because nobody shows up to make the beds on Three.

Hey. Not fair. What about the carpenter slash writer slash bastard that got her into this mess in the first place?

I imagine he's still on his knees in some hotel room, somewhere, fingering the hair trigger on his air-nailer and plotting how to ruin other innocent lives.

Gee. And he seemed like such a nice guy.

Fiction, Loris. Worse than heroin. You stick the needle right in the heart. Anyway, I'd better let you get back to work before Mrs. Windsor shows up and teaches us both something about the suggestion of violence.

———————

That was it. Nothing happened, really. The next day he was finished on Three, moved up to Four, Carole's floor. We exchanged a few words in the elevator, maybe, and then he was gone. They pulled him off, sent him to another job. This fat little guy with a permanent hangover finished off the baseboards on the upper floors.

That was it. At least I *think* that was it. I'm still not sure if he was making a pass at me or what, but the thing is, I've been having a hard time getting to sleep, since. Weird thoughts. I can't talk to Donnie about it.

Just what the hell *is* going on? What am I here for? To make beds, empty ashtrays, make Donnie happy? I guess, maybe, but I find myself picking up those literary reviews lately, and if I ever see any postmodern crap about "Baseboards" under that guy's name, I'll hunt him down and I'll . . .

———————

I *will, too.*

With a hiss, way in the back of her throat, Loris sails the magazine into her fireplace.

Who does he think he is, saddling me with a loyal bread truck of a husband, stealing my voice and blunting it against his own self-importance? It wasn't like that. It wasn't like that at all. The magazine was a trap; I recognized it immediately. The remark about gardening was a joke. And I was the one who suggested the title. He probably doesn't even understand it.

She hunts him. It isn't hard; she uses the white pages. She

pictures him alone and desperate, is disconcerted to find him married and complacent.

You have compromised me, she says, when she finally thinks they are alone.

Sorry about that, he says. He takes her clothes, hangs them on a tree.

The thing about doing baseboards, he says, is that it keeps you humble. The carpenter on his knees, *that* was supposed to be the central image of the story. Somehow it got lost. It was more like *your* voice appropriated *me*.

That ain't my voice, she says, and you wouldn't know humble from cow shit if you landed face down in a nice fresh pie.

That's a good line, he says. Can I use it?

Why start asking me now? You've used just about everything else.

Not quite everything. Not quite yet.

Oh God.

——————

I've tried to be patient. They were like a couple of children, so unsure, so innocent yet so suspicious. I knew, when I married him, that I would always have to share him with *them*, but this one scared me more than the others; she seemed so angry, so confident, so sure of her own right to exist outside his imagination. And the fire she lit in his eyes was one I hadn't seen in so long.

I invited her to tea. I poured. She took her tea pure, no sugar. I took enough for both of us. I've been compensating for a long time.

She had an attractive personality, even with his smell lingering, evanescent, on her flesh. I liked her immediately, which didn't make things any easier.

Don't you understand? I said. You were better off before. At least you had your Donnie.

No, I didn't. He made all that up.

You have to go back, anyway. Where you come from. Where you belong.

Where *do* I come from? Where *do* I belong? What the hell is *really* going on? He never gave me a background. He stripped it all away and left it hanging in some tree. I have to forge ahead, create myself anew. Don't I?

You can't stay here. You are plugging up the process. Why on earth did you come, anyway?

I wanted to hurt him. Because he hurt me.

She dropped her eyes. She could hear how silly she sounded.

Go find your clothes, I said.

It was hopeless, obviously. I sought out Donnie. He wasn't easy to track down; Lenis had salvaged him from the wreckage of another story altogether. Loris was right about him; he didn't really belong here at all. It doesn't matter where you begin or where you end up, either, maybe, but if you wrap yourself around a telephone pole en route. . . .

Donnie was bitter.

I don't know squat about baseboards, he said.

Narrative is linear, by its nature, I said. Like baseboards. The copes and mitres break the line, change the direction of flow; it doesn't matter where you start, where you finish, all the angles add up to nothing in the end. Hopefully enclosing the story.

You're stretching, he said. I just wanted to make her happy. To see her smile. . . .

Go find your *hurt*, Donnie. Find your *anger*. Loris needs you.

He's right, though. I *am* stretching. If I stretch a little further, I can see him: the carpenter on his knees, butting his tape to the corners, scribbling numbers and fractions of numbers on scraps of paper. If I stretch really hard, I can even see his thoughts, crisp and linear, mitred neatly at the corners. He is thinking about Loris, wondering if he has read more into her boisterous laugh than is really there. Or less.

Turn the corner.

On his feet, in the hall at his chop saw, translating the chicken scratches on his slips of paper into accurate lengths of baseboard, marking each measurement carefully on the back of each piece, eyeballing the run of the blade, squeezing the trigger, watching Loris walk away from him down the hall, her arms full of towels.

The saw screams through.

Turn the corner.

His penis thickens, but his thoughts go limp and vague. He is thinking about evolution, the endless striving for complexity. But *is* the double Ph.D. really any *better* than the amoeba or the paramecium? Or just a heck of a lot more complicated? Viruses are elegantly simple, and maybe they are gaining on us. Maybe this complexity bit was just an evolutionary blind alley?

Turn the corner.

On his knees, untangling his feet from the air hose, squeezing a dab of glue on the clean bevel, squeezing the mitre together, squeezing the trigger of the air-nailer. A muffled explosion, a thimbleful of gale force wind, driving the joint together, squeezing out a threadline of excess glue. He wipes it clean with his thumb, wipes his thumb on his coveralls. He is thinking about Loris, bending to make up an endless bed, one ear on her soap opera, both eyes open for clues. Loris, up to her elbows in an eternal toilet, drawing her own conclusions.

Turn the corner.

The carpenter on his knees. Squeezing an open mitre, obsessed with detail, process. All the angles add up to zero. It *does* matter. Where you begin. Where you end up. Consider each room with care. Cut your copes away from the line of the eye. See the whole room first, then each detail, then again the whole. It matters.

113

On his knees, he hardly begins to suspect that I have appropriated *his* voice, now. Who ever heard of a *man* writing a story about vegetables, anyway?

He sits in front of the word processor, picking his feet. The hollow hum of memory, the radiant throb of the cursor. . . .

Complacent. Forgotten where he parked his ambition, that boy. With his Swiss Army knife he hacks away the dead skin around his heels, chews it like gum. Going nowhere. Fast. Someone *had* to step in.

Just to make *him* happy?

The view from up here is better than down on Three. Loris will never see this view. The mountains look like they have been cut out of the sky with a razor knife.

Donnie will take care of her, one way or another.

Into the Crystal Mountains

And we should consider every day lost on which we have not
danced at least once.   —Nietzsche

I'M JUST A HAPPY-GO-LUCKY GUY. All the troubles of my heart have
turned to blood and flowed away, darkening rivers, clouding seas.
Once I cried in my beard, tore my wig, cursed my faith— no more.
. . . I'm just a happy, I'm just a lucky, I'm just a happy-go-lucky guy.
I still have two left feet but I dance every day with angels on the
head of my pain. I was a traveller and all places were the same. . . .
Now the world comes to me and every day is new. I rubbed
shoulders with travellers; we were world-weary together. Nine
lifetimes I lived with no hope of being reborn as anything but a cat.
Now I am reborn every moment. All the troubles of my heart turn
to beer, run down the side of my glass.

*I had a home once, in blackfly country, a crystal palace built of twigs. The red
trout leapt from the streams into my frying pan, the spinach and the asparagus
climbed from the cold earth to steam on my plate. But small men came with
big machines. . . .*

I dream of the dead. Dylan Thomas calls me; I am in the tub. I say to him, Dylan, as I drip on the rug, Why not go lucky into that happy night?

A fire green island in a fire blue sea, a plateau ringed by mountains, ten thousand windmills stand like—windmills . . . the metaphorical imperative recedes . . . Lasithi winter. . . .

I will write a book. I'll call it *The Autobiography of a Happy-Go-Lucky Guy*. I'll set it in type with my teeth, print it on handmade paper in my basement. The walls will sweat. I'll sell it door to door in Saskatoon; surprised wives will stand on bitter January doorsteps; block heaters will throb, warming sluggish oil. . . .

The dying lion of Lucern . . . the living lions of Zurich . . . the Bavarian lion of Nauplion, sleeping in stone . . . the fleabit lion of Reggio Cal, brooding under pizza pasta skies . . . I died nine lives with no hope—but now I'm just a happy-go-lucky, lucky-go-happy, happy-go-lucky guy.

I was the dream taster, sleeping off life in my basement crypt. Now I lie awake nights and sing. There are diamonds in the surf. When the wind stops you can hear the mountains dwindle, turning back into molehills. My children grow away from me. My son learns to use a sword; he knows the names of dead kings. My daughter coaxes the music off the page, makes it dance. I still have two feet left, and daily, with a million angels, I dance in my head.

The word wakes in me like love, kindled between children, thinking themselves old enough. I am old enough. To know better?

I have been absent from the ring a long time, but I still have a chin I can take it on. The word wakes in me like spring in Canada, impossibly slow, but delicious. The snow rots from beneath; the going is treacherous, but the sap in the waking wood is sweet. I'm just a happy-go-lucky guy. No chips on my shoulder.

My origins are obscure. I've been accused of nationalities, never convicted. I've burned my birth certificate; my passport is an elegant forgery. World-weary together, we ride the trains. The Istanbul Express, slower than life on daytime TV. The Turkish border guards inspect our passports by candle light. Clear and empty we ride the trains. The streetlights of south Wales are yellow as pumpkins. Across the water, Ireland waits, green as morning. Offa's Dyke is a ripple in time, Hadrian's Wall a hyphen between unaspirated syllables. Trajan's Column supports the finest single example of modern Italian scaffolding to be seen today. World-weary together. . . .

Stone cold sober on the Turquoise Coast. I'll trade Gorki Park *and* The Bagavad Gita *for anything in English with a plot. We travel to prove to ourselves that all places really are the same. After a while at least the strangeness becomes familiar.*

I haven't always been a happy-go-lucky guy. I cried at sad movies. History turned my stomach; I took reality seriously. I had a home in the woods, once, in blackfly, sandfly, deerfly, horsefly, moosefly, sucked dry mosquito country, and the sweet sap flowed into my bucket. Now my bucket has a whole in it. I lived in the old walled city in a basement room of stone. The walls gleamed with sweat as the heat of endless summer hunkered down. I was a hired killer without work. I devised methods to murder the flies which hid from the heat in my room, my tomb, my crypt. I lived in my dreams and died a thousand deaths, never to be reborn as anything. I lived in dreams and, when dreams ran dry, I travelled blind, into the Crystal Mountains. . . .

When the weather is fine there is work. . . . When there is work there is money for wine. . . . When there is no work there is still money for wine, if for nothing else. . . .

I have not always been. . . . I cried into my radio. My bucket had a hole in it. Drawing dreams from a dry well, wishing on stars as they fell. . . . Holding you close in an empty embrace, kissing the smile from your pretty face. . . . Winter trying to wake us from tropic dreams. . . . Into the mountains, the Crystal Mountains, dwindling to molehills, we flee. Riding the trains, travelling blind, world-weary, together. . . . Dreaming in a leaky caravan . . . Neapolitan haystack . . . The road to Connemara falls away . . . Peeling back time, unwholesome skin, flakes of weather. . . . Stone cold sober on the Turquoise Coast. . . . Rainy days on the Balaton. . . . Hiding from the bells of the old walled cities. . . . All the troubles, bubbles rising in my glass. . . .

My Mantra:
I'mjustahappygoluckyI'mjustahappygoluckyI'mjustahappygolucky guy.

The world wakes in me like love, twinkling between children, old enough. Keeping a hand in. Between the thighs of the night, among the gentle daughters of oblivion. I sit in my place like a man on a precipice; the pretty girls pluck at my liver with razor sharp smiles. The innocence of eagles. . . . Keeping a finger in . . . up the ass of Old Father Time. . . . Humping the camel at both ends. . . . My nose has worn a groove in the grindstone.

I have been running with the windows open, trying to clear the air. No chips, no shoulders, even. . . . When the mouse is away, the cat goes fishing. . . .

The blank page perishes at the first stroke of the pen. Our words of love freeze into swords with which we disembowel each other. I dance on the edge of the precipice. The edge is decked in flowers, but it is still the edge. The ground is soft, but I'm just a guy; the ground is soft; our footprints fill with tears and we drown, but I'm just . . . the ground is soft—the edge is decked—the mountains dwindle—the windmills stand like windmills, Lasithi winter, Saskatoon spring. . . .

I lie awake nights and sing, softly to the hungry dark, my mantra: I'm just a happy, I'm just a lucky, I'm just a guy.

I knew a woman. Our lives grew round each other 'til it was impossible to tell my roots from her branches. We built a crystal palace, in blackfly country, of popsicle sticks and string. Men with no conscience raped us. We fled into the Crystal Mountains; the word woke in me like death. She sat at her wheel and fragments of her broken heart were caught up in the twining yarn. The treadle drew her foot, as life makes us live, in spite of ourselves.

I was not the author of her misfortunes, but I leant my editorial skills.

We travelled blind, and all places were the same, only some places they grew bananas, and it was easier to find a cheap room. Our children grew away from us. They taunted the waves; they gathered the diamonds in the surf. . . . We gathered the oranges that fell from the trees and our lives grew through each other.

Time is just a dream we shared: the sleeping lion of Nauplion, the lemons of Mycenae. . . . Open like windows, the world blows through us. . . .

I'm just a happy-go-lucky guy; time is a thief and so am I. I have no wings, but I can fly, 'cause I'm such a happy-go-lucky guy. Why? What alley did I dump my garbage in? My misery, my grief, my tragic fate? Behind a bush, under a rock, down by the old mill stream? No. I carry all the weight of fate in my back pocket, and still I dance. Watch me. I dance in the aisles of the SuperValu Store. I dance on the mall, in the hall, up the wall. I dance in the middle of Eighth Street, ignore the horns; I laugh at cops and politicians. I dance on the *Globe and Mail* in the morning; the CBC *News* I trample beneath my perfect pas de basque. I dance on the bus, 'til old crippled pregnant ladies, laden with groceries and small children, get up and offer me their seats. I dance in court and when they throw the book at me, I catch it and throw it back. I dance in my cell; in every cell I dance. Listen. Do you hear my steps rattle on the eggshell dreams, shattering in your brain? Do you hear my mantra, echoing, as you mull life like cheap wine? I dance in my wheelchair. I sing in my soundproofed room. I'm just a happy-go

     I'm just a happy-go-

     I'm just a happy-go-

     lucky guy.

My daughter presses flowers between the pages of my book; they fall like tears as I write. My son bakes bread. We betray each other in small ways, which bind us more tightly in webs of fidelity. The cat goes fishing.

We are like the flowers which grow out of the cracks in the wall. Nourished by the dust of centuries, sucking a meager living from fissures in the rock, destroying the civilization which nurtures us with the probing growth of rootlets.

Fill the page, fill the page, the empty places in the heart cannot be filled with words. Create the illusion. Fill the page, stop the hole in your heart with words. . . . Blood, warmer than wine, more nourishing than ice . . . in the essence of the flower, in the twining fibers of the yarn. . . . Life, drawn from us, as the treadle pulls the foot. . . .

I'm just a happy-go-lucky-guy, the fat in the fire, out of the frying pan, dance, dance, the words only dance around the feelings. . . .

Drawing dreams from a dry well; wishing on stars as they fell. Brewing love potions in a wooden shoe, sailing to the moon in a second-hand canoe. . . . The words only dance—the words only dance—the words only dance around the feelings. . . .

Into the mountains, the Crystal Mountains. . . . I had a home once, in waterfall, wildwood flower, whip-poor-will country, and once I lived on a yellow rock in a fire blue sea. The smiling boats of Gozo go; flying fish flee before. The sea moves in all directions at once. Maltese winter, rubbing shoulders, world-weary, together. . . . Stone cold sober by the Blue Lagoon; I'd trade anything in English for a Maltese moon. . . .

The metaphorical imperative deceives. There are diamonds in the rough. The lampuki leap from the sea, into our frying pan. The world wakes in us like sleep.

Shall I show slides of my former lives at the public library? Here is a happy-go-lucky guy, among old stones in a field. Sitting on a menhir under the Carnac sun, smelling the wild narcissus at Hagar Qim, among old stones at Efes, Megalopolis, Eleusis. . . . A world full of old stones. Scratch the words on an old stone in a field: Here Lies a Happy-go-lucky Guy. Happy the Worms that Gorge on his Entrails, Lucky the Microbes that Swim in the Soup of his Sightless Sockets. Happy the Bones, Lucky the Dust. . . .

All the troubles of my life shall turn to dreams. Even my nightmare is a horse of a different colour. . . .

I dream of the dead. Berryman sends me a letter; it goes astray. I have to go down and collect it from the Dead Letter Office. Creepy in here, all the deceased mail laid out on slabs, tags on toes: Misdirected/ No Such Address/ Moved/ Incorrect Postal Code/ Insufficient Postage/ Improper Envelope Format. . . . I make a positive I.D. Yes, this is I: Mr. Happy-Go-Lucky Guy, Poste Restante, Somewhere Among Old Stones in a Field. They let me take it home in a plain pine box. When I open it bones rattle like wind chimes; a couple of bats fly out. (Rabid, probably, one bites me on the ear and I begin to foam.) I hear, writes John, that you are just a happy-go-lucky guy. Myself, I had a most marvelous piece of luck: I died. Luck, I say, has nothing to do with it. Wake up, Henry. Roll over, Mr. Bones; you is snoring. No return address—There is a bridge at the end of the world. I try to follow, but his river has run dry. . . .

Into the Crystal Mountains we flee. Scrounging a meager living from fissures. In the essence of the flowers that grow from the wall, in the twining of vines, growing round each other. . . .

We had a home in spruce bud worm, gypsy moth, acid rain country. Small men with big machines came and raped our dream, made of a living forest a small dead pile of money. . . .

We flee, Lasithi winter, Olympian spring; there are avalanches on the throne of the gods, adders in the underbrush. We drink the clearest waters in the world.

We had a home built of spit and plywood. When the wolf came to the door, we asked him in. My, what big eyes you have, we said, buying all his lottery tickets. What lovely furry ears, we said, giving him all our old bottles, bundling our papers in the back of his van. We admired his teeth and promised to read every word of Awake and The Watchtower. He went off whistling, with his tail between his teeth. When the Prince of Darkness came to make us an offer, I locked him in the outhouse. For months we kept him there, living on ashes and toilet paper. We had to shit in the woods. Please, he begged, through the new moon window, I have things to do, responsibilities. Who's going to look after Hell while I'm away? Have you any idea how long it takes to get that fire going, if once you let it go out? My heart bleeds, I said. See, blood, warmer than wine, more nourishing than ice. In the end I let him go with a scolding. Bet you can't even dance, I said. I've got two left hooves, he said, but I piped him back to Hell, doing a hornpipe, his tail between his teeth like a rose. I am not cruel. Just happy-go-lucky.

I was not always so. I've had my upside downs; I've visited the nuisance grounds. I even flirted with suicide, but her shoulders were cold. . . . I tried to shoot myself—the curling iron wasn't loaded. Hanged myself in the basement, bust a water pipe, nearly drowned. In the end I hired a hit man. Gave him half the cash up front—I think he's living in Florida, now. That's cool. . . . Ten thousand lifetimes on the head of a pin, in the eye of the hurricane, I've danced. After eternity, even the worst weather gets boring. I've danced on the lip of the volcano, on the fault line where drifting continents crash together. After eternity, even cataclysm smacks of anti-climax. That's cool. . . . You know the refrain—sing it with me:

> I'm
> Yes I'm
> Oh, Mama, Daddy, Baby you know that
> I'm just a happy
> Goddamn, I'm a happy
> I'm a happy, I'm a lucky, I'm a go
> I'm a guy . . .
> well,
> most of the time. . . .

I know it's a long shot in the cold dark. . . . Bright-eyed and bushy-toothed, the killer lurks in his basement. The walls sweat. Heat stalks the street; automobiles melt. The killer paints his windows black. He is fond of cows. The heat kills dogs, tortures the grass that grows in the cracks of the pavement. The killer watches the walls drip and dreams of pastures. Good weather to make hay. Cut in the morning, rake after dinner, bale before dark. Drink a gallon of beer and sleep under the stars. The killer sleeps in his crypt and dreams of gentle Jerseys, with soft eyes and smooth, full udders. He has a thousand ways of killing flies. The flies drink from the bleeding walls and breed on his contempt. Bright-eyed, bushy-toothed, he constructs infernal machines for their destruction. He guillotines them with a rusty razor blade, garrotes them with dental floss, blasts them out of the air with rubber bands. He dreams of milk, cream rising. . . . Hiding from bells in the old walled city, killing to live, dancing in the well, wishing on starlings as they fly. He has lived in the depths, a miserable, a luckless guy. He has combed the nuisance grounds, down in the dumps, and the mouth, living on slugs and wild garlic, the poor man's *escargot*.

Drawing dreams from a poisoned well, wishing on bones. All the hungers of his life, turning to thirst, Death Valley in the back of his throat, Sahara in his heart. . . . His mantra is unprintable. Bats hang from the rafters of his soul like broken black umbrellas. Tears freeze as they fall. He's dancing on thin ice. It's all a front, this happy luck, deep down inside he suffers, bleeds, blood, redder than wine, more nourishing than nice. . . .

He never saw the black gates of Dyarbakir, turned back by the endless steppes, flatter than Saskatchewan, where no flower blooms and a zillion bees fly a quintillion kilometers, to steal a drop of honey from each other. He never made it into the Crystal Mountains. The passes were closed, avalanches on the throne of the gods, adders in the underbrush. The bare arms of Lasithi windmills could not hold him. The smiling boats of Gozo left him scrounging for diamonds in the surf.

A sham, a dancer out of step, treading on the toes of angels, falling off the head of a bent pin. Every day lost. A long shot—the cold dark. He only bets on shots so long, even when you win, you lose. Even a happy-go-lucky guy can get the blues.

Like a car thief in the night , I hotwire my own heart. Wishing on storks . . . dripping on the rug . . . why not go happy . . . luck has nothing. . . . Sure I bleed. The treadle draws the foot. Yes, my pain is vast; it has no horizons, flatter than Saskatchewan; a googolplex of killer bees search my skin for a spot that's yet to feel a sting. Yes my mantra rings hollow, but it rings. And every day is lost, anyway. And when I dance, out of sync, out of step, my two left feet treading on each other's toes, all the lies on my conscience turn to truth and fly away.

And if I melt my wings of wax, and I must be untrue to the sky, I'll dance with squid and shellfish in the dark of the sea. Because I'm just a happy, a happy-go-lucky, I'm just a happy-go-lucky me.

Falling

24

FALLING. INTO HER EYES? WHO FELL?

Who flew?

If I were to write a story, this story, again, I might be inclined to begin at the end, work my way back to the beginning.

———————

23

Alia falls asleep at her desk. She dreams they are playing for her clothes. They smoke and the differences between them begin to dissolve. She can read the flaming script in their thought balloons. The stones they place on her body divide her like a kingdom.

———————

22

Alia knows that if she *had* slept with Neely, she wouldn't have been able to come back here tonight, to play this scene straight. Just holding the fragrant flowers close to her skin has lit a fire in her. She is almost sorry Neely only wanted fifty dollars and the name of the dentist they used to visit.

Through the sliding glass doors she watches them, leaning over the parapet wall, passing the joint, Jordan turning to point out the mountains, the bridges, the crimes of passion spilling into the empty streets below.

Alia sits at her desk and looks at her novel. Not at the cardboard boxes full of printouts and notes and files; all that is compost, a mere apprenticeship, preparing her for this. She sees the novel, floating just above the desk, a slim compact volume full of dark possibilities, a compendium of perfect details, each carefully dovetailed into the whole.

She can taste it now. It all happens in the minds of her two protagonists, while their bodies are otherwise (but mutually) occupied. The voices, quite separate and distinct at first, begin to blur and run together as the narrative pace accelerates and the rhythm builds to a climax.

She sees it all there, floating, pressed tight between the pages. She will write it tomorrow. After she writes the letter to Jordan, telling him why she can't work for him any more.

———————

21

Just the smell of the herb she carries is almost too much for Alia. She digs it out of her panties and tosses it beside Jordan's little pile of captured black stones. She wonders if they have exchanged a word the whole time she's been gone. Her eyes stray to the mess in the kitchen.

There's some burgers left, says Jordan, digging in his pouch for cigarette papers. They kinda fell apart but they were okay, weren't they, Kit?

I had pizza with Neely, says Alia.

On my time?

It was part of the deal.

He weighs the bag in his hand, crumbling the bud a little, then holding it under his nose.

What else was part of the deal?

You said you didn't want me to bother you with details.

That's right. Come on, Kit. Let's go out on the roof and see if we can smoke this.

———————

20

Alia finds them locked over the stones.

Kit has not noticed before how graceful she is. The perfume of the skunkweed in her panties fills the penthouse like sudden lust. She is flushed, but she carries herself with a power and assurance he hasn't noticed before. It reminds him of his mother. He feels nothing. Nothing.

———————

19

I'm going to charge him. Now that Mom's dead.

What? Charge who?

Lee.

Lee? Charge him for what, for God's sake?

What he did to me. To us.

I don't—

You really didn't know, did you?

Lee?

You thought you knew him, didn't you?

How long—I mean—

As long as I can remember. I don't know about since I left. Tree is still there. Ko.

Jordan looks at the black and white stones, so carefully placed at the intersecting points of the black grid on the green board. He knows that somewhere in his brain he has stored the information he needs to interpret the symbolism here, but right now he is wondering how long it is going to be before he regains access to those files.

He leans back and reaches for his beer, which is still empty.

18

Falling headfirst, at best, more likely at some oblique angle to the plane of the reflecting glass. Each image that explodes across his consciousness is stretched and shattered by momentum.

Perhaps, falling, he falls into someone, finds that all the flickering images are only reflections in her eyes.

But whose? Who fell?

Who flew?

17

If I were writing a novel I could stretch here. Reach. Flashback. Scenes of J's childhood, his dominance over his brothers, his fierce jealousy of their ability to remain complacent. His own tendency toward chronic anguish and hopeless love. Sketches of his parents: his father kind, human, but frail, addicted to reading and reticence; his mother a workaholic martyr, turning her husband's small family monument business into a highly successful one-stop shopping center of death. I could detail the anguish of his flight, and the ecstasy of finding Joy in the streets.

It was Lee talked her out of having the abortion, not me. I knew, right then, that I'd lost her. I kept my mouth shut. She said she couldn't handle a baby, not yet, and I knew she could handle anything, but I said nothing, I told myself it wasn't my place, it was her body, her decision. It was a trap, a trick, but it told the truth. I was always more than willing to silence my heart for love. And it always cost me. . . .

———————

16

The burgers crumble, but they are delicious. Kit puts ketchup on his. Jordan finishes the beer.

Damn it, he says, I'm sorry, Kit. I'm sorry I couldn't be your father. Always too damn full of myself. Nothing's really changed, has it?

Mom's dead.

That's not your fault, either.

Good burgers, Jordan.

Alia will find them locked over the stones.

———————

15

Not Jordan, up to his elbows in tofu-burgers.

Get that for me, would you, Kit?

Alia's voice, breathless, far-away. *I have to talk to him.*

She says she has to talk to you.

Not right now. Tell her I'm busy. What does she want, anyway? I sent the girl on a simple errand.

Tell him I found what he wants but he may not be happy about the price.

Kit repeats this. Jordan laughs. Damn the price.

He says damn the price.

I think I'd really better speak to him.

Maybe call him back. He's cooking.

Cooking? Oh my God.

Tell her I don't care what it costs, Jordan calls, over his shoulder. Tell her not to bother me with details.

He says—
I heard him.

14

If I *were* to write a novel (I mean, hey, the Carpenters' Union hasn't
called me and now Carolyn is working nights as a welder) it would
be wonderful, a cut crystal of a book, every facet gleaming. Set with
the vivid unreal depth of a hologram against a backdrop of the
twisted landscape of contemporary urban legend.

I see a character, a consciousness, in flight, or, more precisely,
in fall.

Falling. They say your whole life flashes, reflected in the flickering windows, each reflection another story. . . .

Time slows to a crawl, or disconnects entirely, the main spring
sprung. With the tension of chronology released, moments drift
past, behind the flashing windows.

They say your whole life flashes. I never understood that. I
thought time was a wire of infinite length and infinitesimal thick-
ness, but maybe time is more of a soup, chunky. . . .

In the rising distance the hopeless rule the streets, their faces
smeared with the flesh of their aborted children, sharing their
green M+M's with hairy-armed hitchhikers.

But who is falling? And why? And is that really the street rushing
up to greet your mug or only the slap in the face of waking?

Somebody had better get that phone.

13

Dark and light, encircling each other. Kit places another stone.
Jordan feels the wire tighten.

You must be hungry, he says. That is, I'm hungry.

In the kitchen they find beer. Kit holds one and watches Jordan pretend he knows his way around his own kitchen. A bold and messy performance. He bangs cupboards and roots in refrigerator drawers; he questions his son, as he had been unable to do, face to face, over tea or over a game of go.

So. What line of work are you in, then?

I'm a thief.

Jordan pulls his beard out of the fridge.

A thief?

A burglar. Breaking and entering. It's a skilled trade. You have to know your shit.

Jesus, man, you can't be serious. Or maybe you can? Why not? Hell, I claim to make a living standing up in front of people and making fun of myself. Hardly a skilled trade. But hey, a burglar, that's something I guess. Self-employed, then? Ever get busted?

I'm good. I always work alone. Nobody to fuck up, to let you down, to talk too much. Also I can run very fast.

That hasn't changed. But *you're* talking to *me*.

You don't know if anything I've told you is true. And I haven't told you anything important. Like where I live or the name I'm using, now.

Jordan piles fruits and vegetables on the counter, grates tofu into a bowl, chops onions 'til his eyes swim.

No, he says. That isn't what's important.

The phone.

12

Jordan sends Alia out for marijuana.

What?

I said I'm out of weed. Pick us up some, will you?

Alia does as she is told. This is the specific nature of the contract. Sometimes she argues, and always there has been a line he would never dare to cross, but tonight there is something dangerous in his mood. She doesn't argue.

This isn't one of her normal duties. He knows she doesn't use the stuff, though he doesn't know why. She knows he has a source, a native guy with a pager who drives pizza. Jordan calls him often. But Jordan doesn't offer her the number. She is sure this is a test, but of what? All she can do, as always, is improvise.

The only person she can think of who might be able to get drugs on short notice is Neely, her ex-boyfriend. She gets this curious, ironic tingle, thinking that in order to fulfill Jordan's orders she may have to offer Neely something more personal than cash. The bottom falls out of the elevator.

11

That would be me, and even though I'm not in Maui anymore and I've come home from holidays to find myself laid off, I promised myself (and Carolyn) that I wouldn't write any more novels 'til I sold one of the first nine, and if I go and ask Tree this thing will be out of control for sure.

10

Tree has had the hardest time of all, I think. Did Karma tell you he tried to— kill himself?

No. Karma's smart and Tree is suicidal. Everything sure changed after I left, didn't it?

It's not your fault.

I know that. I can't take the blame for Tree being suicidal any more than I can take the credit for Karma turning out to be smart. I never mattered much when I was there. I don't guess my leaving made a lot of difference.

It—

It what?

I was going to say it broke your mother's heart. But that's neither true nor fair.

Tell him the truth then, Alia is thinking. *Tell him it broke your heart. Or maybe that isn't true or fair, either. Maybe what Kit says is true, though how he can sit there and say it and place another stone on another intersection. . . .*

Maybe somebody should ask Tree.

9

Alia is frustrated as hell. If *she* were writing this story it would be different. These stupid men would be reaching inside and pulling it out by the handful, dumping it on the table. There are scenes in her novel which bring tears to her eyes, even though she hasn't written them yet.

She wants to scream or watch TV or something. Neither would be acceptable. She sits at her desk and sorts through her In-basket, but there is nothing there that does not dissolve into despair when she looks at it.

8

It is a game of territory, space, control. Kit remembers learning the game from a friend, bringing it home and teaching Jordan to play in the guts of the mill as wooden gears clacked and groaned, and the heavy grind-stones shushed together, filling the air with an ocean of tiny noise, fine as flour.

This was Jordan's territory, the heavy hand-built hardwood cogs and gears were his handiwork and his bailiwick. More and more, Lee and Joy concentrated their efforts on the tea room, the marketing of Old Mill souvenirs, the packaging of the stone-ground organic wheat and rye and barley in decorative cotton sacks, for the tourists. Jordan lived inside his machinery, more and more, a bearded gnome in coveralls, white as an old man, grunting at flashbulbs, reading Ouspensky and Suzuki, his space as clearly defined as if a row of shiny white stones delineated the boundaries.

In the beginning it was a dream, shared. A vision. He wants to tell this one good thing to his son, as if, after all that has happened since, it might still make a difference.

It was Joy's money, he says, placing a white stone. But the three of us shared the vision. Turning that derelict ruin of a place back into a working mill, capturing the gravity stored in all that falling water, using that pull to lift ourselves out of the darkness. Even then we felt the darkness closing in, though we were so young.

Kit fondles the black stones. He places each with a careful dispassionate deliberation. Jordan feels a constriction in his chest.

For a long time I couldn't sleep, Kit says. Without the sound of the water.

———

7

After tea they play go. Alia, in the kitchen choking over the dishes, is shocked breathless by how rapidly their embarrassment has degenerated into a competitive struggle. She has always refused Jordan's attempts to lure her into the contests which obsess him: go, chess, backgammon, sex.

Kit fondles the black stones, perfectly calm, unconcerned, alone in the world.

Alia holds onto the refrigerator, feels its throb envelop her.

———

6

Every gesture, every simple action of the hands, is full of meaning.

Alia is, by this time, as familiar with the *chanoyu*, the way of tea, as Jordan himself, but this is something different, an agreement, not a ritual. Something perhaps as simple as an agreement not to disengage.

Jordan pours. The tea is clear and light.

I never got to see your show, says Kit.

I know that. Do you imagine I don't know that? Didn't I look into every pair of eyes in every audience for over two years, looking. . . . Knowing you wouldn't come. Why should you? You always could smell a crock.

I was going to go. I just never got it together.

I was going to write a follow-up hit, something visceral but not too heavy, that's what my agent said. I just never quite got it together, did I, Alia?

Your father has been having a difficult period, creatively, says Alia, hating the words as she speaks them, hollow, like wood riddled with insects. Ever since. . . .

Ever since his first wife died. Just like that. Abruptly abdicating her fair share of the blame. Left him high and dry, her first husband, certainly, but morally unable to declare himself, one way or the other, with respect to anything else in the world.

––––––––––

5

Alia makes tea. Alia is second oldest of four daughters, the only one still unmarried. She is on speaking terms with her parents, who live in Winnipeg. She has a master's degree in Fine Arts and has been writing a novel for years. She is, ostensibly, Jordan's personal secretary. She took the job because the first time she saw his one man show: *The Last Living Hippie Sets the Record Straight*, she knew he was a genius. She keeps it because he pays her, because he keeps his hands off her, and because he needs her.

She likes to be needed. She still knows that he is a genius, but she is no longer sure that genius is either admirable or desirable.

Why did Jordan hire her? Because he never learned how to type. He keeps her on because he is in love with her.

Alia is good at tea, as at most things. It is important to her to do things well. Perhaps this is why genius escapes her. She may never finish the novel.

4

I write this in a Mexican hammock between two trees I don't know the names of on the shady side of the Kipihulu Campground, southeastern Maui. No shit. The living volcanos of the big island are obscured by cloud this afternoon, but this morning the view was "killer," to borrow the idiom of our neighbour Jamie, a homeless, unemployed, dispossessed guitarist and apprentice tile- setter from California.

In such a time and place it is difficult to bring to bear the emotional leverage necessary to write the scene which must follow here, to describe the feelings generated when the father lays eyes on the son he lost a whole lot longer ago than he even imagines.

Here, in eastern Maui, the mangos are falling to dent the hoods of the rental cars. For a decent papaya you have to shake the tree a little.

Imagine a place where all the things you have lost in your life are gathered together in a heap. Every wallet and watch and wedding ring, every key, of course, but also every opportunity, every illusion.

Imagine stumbling upon this place when you are only looking for a way out of the building.

Maybe that's how Jordan felt, when Kit appeared behind Alia's bicycle in the doorway. I don't know, and I'm the one making this up. Today, I just can't shake the tree any harder.

3

The last living hippie sits cross-legged in his penthouse prison, sanding the bishop and trying to remember Maui.

Specifically, he is trying to hold in the vise of his mind a single image, culled from the flotsam of his last days on the beach at Makena. He can describe the image to himself in intimate detail; the co-ordinates of the curve of that unknown woman's buttock, as she bent to adjust a sandal strap, are plotted in his brain to a tolerance so fine it hurts. But he cannot hold such spectacular geometry, and the waves break all around him.

The last living hippie is losing his grip.

Jordan knows the bitch will be back soon with the groceries. He will hear the elevator, and draw his robe back around himself and pretend he is meditating. Alia sees through him, and he knows it, but when you have nothing left but pretense, you make the most of it.

Jordan masturbates more now, in his forties, than he ever dared in his teens. But he hasn't had an orgasm since his first wife died. (Since his *first* wife died? As if there might ever be another?) He doesn't jack off any more, he just jacks. Choking the chicken, sanding the bishop. If he could let himself think for a single moment of the bitch queen, Alia, dropping her jeans, he could fill the penthouse with rivers of cum. But he is in love with her, and so he pumps the handle and makes eyes in his mind at every gorgeous woman he has never loved.

The well is dry.

2

Only because. He ran into his karma.

Alia pushes her bicycle into the elevator. The skinny guy with the dark eyes reminds her of somebody. He doesn't look dangerous; a stiff wind might test his respect for gravity. Still, she keeps the bicycle between them. Which means she can't reach the buttons.

The penthouse, please, she says.

He doesn't move, just looks at her, and for a moment she is alarmed, but then she sees that the central button at the top is already aglow. Another moment of panic as the doors hiss shut and she feels his eyes penetrate.

Excuse me, she says. You know Jordan never receives visitors when he's working.

He smiles as if this is a private joke between them. As if he knows that Jordan hasn't been able to work for months, or as if he understands every intimate detail of the role she plays as intermediary between that wonderful insufferable man and the whole demanding imposing bulk of the world.

He'll receive me, he says. When she hears his voice she knows. But why should she blush?

1

It is only because he runs into Karma on Hastings Street that he knows their mother is dead.

Joy, naked, up to her knees in the black roiling water below the mill. Joy, in the kitchen, throwing flour at her two husbands, laughing like laughter was her own invention. Joy, serving blackberry tea to the tourists in her flowered hippie skirts.

Joy, rocking him in her arms when he woke in sweats, still trying to hold the wire that ran through every dream, slicing dark and daylight with the same edge.

Joy, dead, ashes.

Kit knows, for the first time, that he really is alone in the world.

He almost doesn't know his little brother, with the earring and the six-foot wrestler's frame, the sweatshirt with the University crest. Karma is majoring in biology, on a scholarship, and everyone at the University knows him by his middle name, Leon. He plays bass in a post-industrial band called Xyphoid Process.

Lee and Tree are still at the mill, he tells Kit. They closed the tea shop, after Mom died. Lee still does his seminars and shit. Jordan hung around for maybe a year after you split. Mom was pretty freaked. You could have called her or something.

I heard about Jordan's show.

The Last Living Hippie thing. I thought it was pretty stupid, myself, but I guess he made some serious bread off of it. He was at Mom's funeral. Haven't seen him since.

Jordan was the first of Joy's two husbands. Karma and Tree were Lee's sons.

Kit did try to call home, once, three months into the darkness, the second time he got beat up. He wanted to hear his mother's voice; the wire was cutting both ways, slicing his dreams to ribbons.

When Jordan answered the phone, he hung up.

Now she is dead. Ashes since last year. Ashes in the cold black roiling waters below the old mill.

Kit goes home to his tiny room and feels nothing.

After the Fall

ADAM IS BAKING BREAD. He likes to watch the yeast reproducing. He whistles and I know he is thinking about Lilith, his first wife. She was a barren woman, made of storms and meadow mist, but she owns a part of him still, a part I could never even rent. We know these things, now.

He is good with the boys, but they *will* fight.

I take a bath. I like to float in water as warm as my blood and watch my small hairs swim against the ripples. Adam is singing to the hungry yeast. He sounds happy, but I know he blames me still.

It is better this way. We were never faithful, only stupid. Now we are bound together by the hurts we impose on each other.

My body is still smooth and glistens in the fading light. But I can feel my age, settling like gold in my bones. I shall become valuable, and wise, inevitable, and dead.

Adam gets his hands into it. I don't like the way the sticky dough clings to fingers, tenacious as memory. He doesn't seem to mind; he likes the resilience, the way the dough fights back against his hands.

There are things we never speak of. But we know. We appreciate each other, in small ways that transcend resentment. It is better. I know it hurts him that I have found work and he must labour in the search that brings only disappointments. I, at least, have something to show. But he knows I will not leave him again.

The bread becomes a creature. He massages it and it responds to him. A sensual relationship. But I know he will betray it, consign it to the fire, that we may live.

So it is with all of us.

The bath water cannot resist the wonderful temptation of the drain.